THE WINTER KILL

A Medieval Mystery

J R TOMLIN

Albannach Publishing

Created with Vellum

BOOK DESCRIPTION

Thieves and the unsavory of Perth: All in a day's work for lordless Sir Law Kentour...until a mysterious death in the midst of a Highland blizzard. When the sheriff of Perth demands that Sir Law show that the death was not an inconvenient murder, Law thinks this looks like an easy job. But circumstances seem to conspire against him, and another murder follows. Soon the king's chancellor becomes involved, making the mystery even more dangerous. Not only does the murder investigation keep running into brick walls, his friend Cormac plunges into danger; and he once more encounters the thief who has already been a thorn in his side. When answers start to emerge, Sir Law gets more than he bargained for.

FOREWORD

This novel is set in Scotland, hence in it, mainly in dialogue, I use some words, phrases, and spellings native to Scotland. Most are included in the Kindle dictionary or easily understandable in context. You will also find a glossary most of words you may not be acquainted with at the end of the novel.

1

One day after it was ended and over, Sir Law Kintour realized that he and Jannet Neyn Patrik Ross had trudged through the snow on the same day and perhaps at the same hour—although miles apart. Wind had whipped both of them raw on that harsh Scottish November day. But at that moment, he had never heard of her or the house near which she died.

By the time he contemplated this quirk of fate, he could see it happening in his mind. Like an unseen watcher on a nearby mountain, he saw her grasp her thick cloak as she rushed out the narrow doorway. There was a dark shape behind her as she ran down the path. Her hair was honey-gold and whipped in the wind, entangling snowflakes in its strands; her fair, narrow face and long neck gave her a look of vulnerability. She bent forward as she ran into swirling gusts of white, a woman escaping, headlong, from Satan.

From his vantage point, he saw her look over her shoulder and open her mouth to scream. She ran until she struggled through the blowing snow, and he saw how it was done to her.

She'd had no chance at all. He watched her go still, unmarked and sprawled facedown, while snow drifted to cover her body like a shroud. Then there was only the howl of the wind.

But that day as she ran, Law's job was catching a stringy, young man from Lothian named Richerd Ancraft. The lad had found a good position at the house of the Bishop of Dunkeld, running errands for the steward, Nicholl of Annand. Now Nicholl believed the young man was stealing small items—gloves and things of that ilk—to sell. They'd even searched him for contraband but found nothing. The steward wanted the matter resolved quietly, with no embarrassment to himself before the bishop. The steward had paled at the thought, muttering that the bishop was a relation to the king. Having hired a thief would make him look like a fool, and Richerd had been cunning enough not to get caught.

The bishop's man had hired him for this, because, Law realized with bitterness, he looked enough like the rough workers that he would not be noticed amongst them. His natural skin tone was fair but weathered from years in the sun. His light hair was a bit ragged, and his limp might make him look helpless. A closer look at his deep chest and wide shoulders, however, might disabuse the observer of that notion. He'd left his sword in his room at the inn, since no workman would carry such a weapon, but the long dirk at his belt would serve as well. He'd try not to be seen, but if he were, the quarry would not take him for one of the bishop's well-liveried servants. That was a certainty.

Law had been detailed to catch the man red-handed, so the steward could solve the problem with minimal awkwardness with his employer. So Law slipped out of his own room above the inn well before dawn. He wrapped his feet in an extra layer of cloth, before stomping on his boots, for winter had set in. With luck, the buildings would cut off the worst of the weather. But with his heavy wool doublet and thick, dark cloak, even the chill would not keep him from his task.

Sunrise was turning louring clouds to waves of pewter and slate. In the murk of early day, a light fall of snowflakes blew in the wind. He took the narrow Cutlog Vennel through the middle of Perth, and the smell of the wood that was carried through it to be milled blended with the stench of piss. Law reached South Street and followed it to the bishop's house, a block from Watergate Street. He pressed his back to the wall, clapped his hands, and rubbed them together. Already, his fingertips felt numb, but he pulled his cloak closed and his hood up. Law hoped that the quarry would leave soon on his errand to the market, as he did every week for the bishop's all-male household. Law had to detect how the man sneaked goods out of the house.

Richerd was so intent on watching over his shoulder as he slipped from the stair tower at the front of the house that he didn't even notice Law watching. When the man sneaked out of sight, into a tiny alleyway, Law straightened and strolled in the same direction. He slumped and dragged his feet, like a workman on his reluctant way to a day's labor. In the alley, Richerd pushed an empty barrel against the wall, hopped onto it, and reached overhead to untie a bag hanging from a window by a rope. He jumped down, staggered, and fumbled to keep from dropping the loot onto the wet ground.

Law was running toward the culprit, sliding his dirk out of his belt. He rammed his shoulder into Richerd's side and slammed him into the wall.

The youth gave a yelp. "Let me go!"

Law leaned into him, holding him against the wall with his shoulder, and put the dirk to his neck. "I'll have that bag. Now."

"I...I...I'm the bishop's man." Richerd gulped. "He'll have your head!"

Law snorted as he lifted his weight from Richerd just enough to grab the bag from his grip.

Richerd whimpered. "Let me go. I'll pay you...everything that I have. Just let me go."

He trapped the young thief against the wall, again, with his weight in order to sheath his dirk. He then jerked the trembling youth around to twist his arm behind his back. "Back in you go. The steward can deal with you."

He shoved the scrawny lad before him up the stairs to the bishop's door and gave it a kick because his hands were occupied. A servant opened the door. The steward, a small, neat man in an old-fashioned, knee-length tunic laced up the front, motioned him in. Law shoved the young miscreant at them. He tossed the little bag of booty to the beaming steward. "Hanging out the window from a cord high enough overhead that no one would notice—especially in the half-dark."

The steward opened the bag and shook his head. "This is what I needed to take him before the sheriff."

By this time, Richerd was sniveling with tears dripping down his face. "You dinnae pay me enough to take care of my mam and my four sisters. And if I'm in a dungeon, they'll starve."

"You should have thought of their starving before you stole from the bishop," the steward snapped.

He counted out coins from his purse, three merks, as though each came out of his hide, and dropped them into Law's outstretched hand. At the door, Law glanced once over his shoulder at the pathetic scene. To think he'd once been a feared knight. Now he defeated bawling youths.

He walked through battering gusts of snow to the inn and slammed the door closed. When Cormac looked up from where he sat plucking his harp, Law gave him a glower and sat, back against the wall. He motioned to Wulle Cullen, the innkeeper from whom he rented a room above the inn, to bring him a cup of ale.

Wulle looked at him thoughtfully. "What is chewing your arse? Did they nae pay you?"

"They paid." He shook his head. "I've had enough of this kind of thing—as much as I can stand. I caught the sleekit thief, but he was a sniveling lad, nothing more. I dinnae ken if his story of a starving mam was true, but I'm fed up to my neck with it. Is this the only way for me to keep from starving? There must be something that is worth doing." He wondered what it would take to wash away the stink of months of living hand to mouth, bullying petty thieves for merchants.

"A man does what he must to keep food in his belly."

"That cannae be right, Wulle. Many a thing I'd starve before I would do. Bad leg or no, I'm a good hand with a sword and still have a mind that works. I'd put them to good use, but this kind of work sickens me."

Wulle sat a cup of ale down in front of Law. "Drink that down. It'll cure what ails you. And go down the vennel to Mother Dickson's—" He winked. "—for a bit of bobbing before the snow is too deep to make it yon."

Law looked up from staring into the dark ale to see Cormac with a wry tilt to his mouth. He upended his cup, to slurp it down. He paused when Mall Cullen whacked her husband on the back of his head with a spoon.

"You leave that talk to the customers, man. Sir Law has more sense than to waste his coin on a light skirt, any road."

Cormac bent over his clarsach to hide his laughter.

"It's no joke," Law protested. "I must find something that makes me feel that my life isn't a waste."

He leaned his elbows on the rough wood table and tasted the malty brew, caught in a torment he could not define. He knew from the burning in his gut that he would not survive much longer as the same man if he didn't find some meaning in his life again. He needed prideful work that used his skills and abilities. He had once had that—and a companion who meant something to him, to go with it. It was a bitter draught that he'd had a life most men dreamed of: the gold spurs of a knight; a friend to hold his back and to be company for long nights in camp; and a strong lord to follow into battle against their enemies. All of that had drained into the dirt with their lifeblood.

Cormac straightened and strummed a soft, rippling tune. "It meant so much? Fighting for some lord who'd ride any of us down if we stepped in their way?" Cormac had little use for lords unless they would hand over silver for a song.

Law sighed. "It meant I had a place in the world. A task to set my hand to."

"It seems to me this is nae such a bad place in the world to be." Cormac scowled over his harp, and he gave a sudden, discordant strum. "You still have nightmares about dying in battle. About blood and death... That is what you want to go back to? Fighting and killing for some lord who kicked you aside like a dog?"

"It's nae that simple. Fighting... it was what I was raised to do. All that I ken."

"So you want to go back to killing?"

Law twisted in his seat. No, killing was never something he had wanted to do, just his duty.

Cormac shook his head. "And some here might even care if you are alive on the morrow."

Wulle opened his mouth to comment. At Law's glare, he paused but then went on and said, "You're being an idiot."

Outside the wind howled. Law sighed. "Aye, there's no telling how long this storm will last, so bring a pitcher of ale and at least keep me company even if I'm an idiot." He still felt adrift in the world, but that was no reason to take his ill-temper out on them. He shared a pitcher of ale with Cormac, Wulle, and Mall. Then they shared another. Through the night and much of the next day, the wind howled down from the mountains, and outside, snow piled into high drifts.

2

When Law pried his eyes open, slats of light striped his chamber. Pounding on his door blended with thrumming in his head. He lurched to his feet, stumbled to the door, and jerked it open. Sergeant Meldrum, his torso tightly bundled in his plaid and his silver mustache encrusted with ice, raised his hand to knock again.

"What's the to-do?" Law demanded.

"Sir Law," he said, stepping across the threshold. "The lord sheriff bids you hie to the Tolhouse."

"What? Why?" Law rubbed at his eyes, head muzzy.

The man grimaced. "They found a dead woman outside North Street Port, and there's a to-do about it. The sheriff wants you yon."

"A dead woman..." Law repeated. "Someone I know? I ken nothing about a dead woman."

"He did nae say why he wants you, but you'd best go before he's so wroth he commands my men to drag you yon," said the man. He motioned to the melting snow that dripped from his plaid and puddled around his feet. "The snow has stopped falling, but it's deep. You'll want your plaid. But hurry. I dinnae ken how long the lord sheriff will wait."

Law nodded with reluctance. "I suppose I'd better." The water in his ewer was rimmed with ice. When he splashed his face, it cleared some of the fog from his head. He took his cloak from its hook on the wall and wrapped his plaid over it.

In the narrow vennel, wind had sculpted the snow into hills and vales of blinding white. He floundered and ploughed through snow-clogged streets to the dour, massive, gray stone Tolhouse.

By the time he stepped through the arched doorway, his feet were numb lumps of ice. In the main hall of the Tolhouse, most of the burgh's official business went on. Beneath a tapestry of an armored lord cheerfully thrusting his spear into an enemy's breast stood Sir William Ruthven of Balkernoch. He was lord sheriff of the royal burgh of Perth. His arms were crossed over his burly chest, and his face was clenched like a fist. His furious gaze met Law's.

On a trestle table in the middle of the vaulted room lay a cadaver draped with linen. There should have been an assize in session to judge her death, whether natural or no, but except for a guard at the door and a brown-robed priest, Sir William stood on the dais with only a middling man of medium build, medium thinness and sparse, medium-brown hair. The man swung his arms about as he spoke with a kind of angry dismay. "Saint Peter's bones, I tell you she did nae do it," the man told Ruthven as Law approached.

Sir William appeared unmoved as he replied, "There is nae a mark on her, Patrik Ross. Either unhinged she wandered into the storm, or it was self-murder."

"She was of sound mind. Ask anyone who kent her. They'll tell you so."

"If she was nae unhinged, she did it deliberately. She had

cause for despair, or she would nae have run off from her husband. You admitted it, man."

Ross turned to look at the linen-draped corpse. He crossed himself, his body sagging and his face pale as whey. "I telt you that she wrote to me. Maister Kennedy had agreed to help her send her case to the Holy Father, for it was true that there was consanguinity. The cost of a dispensation was great, so we...ignored it when her marriage was negotiated. Even if there was little chance of a divorce..." He choked. "She'd nae do that. To have nae burial rites and spend eternity in Hell." He straightened and glared at the sheriff. "I tell you, someone harmed her. Why would she have been running through a snowstorm? That makes nae sense."

Ruthven gave a derisive snort. "Why would a priest like Kennedy help her send a petition to the Pope? It is a costly matter." He sneered at Ross. "Out of respect to your... cousin...the Lord of the Isles, I'll delay the verdict of the assize, but it cannae be delayed more than a few days."

Ross must have been only a distant cousin of the powerful Lord of the Isles, judging by the sneer, but still a cousin of some sort, Law decided. But he wasn't about to listen to them quarrel all the day. "Aye, but what does all this have to do with me?"

"Naught, but you did well enough with the matter of de Carnea's murder those few months back. I dinnae have the time to deal with such nonsense, but I give you leave to look into it for Sir Patrik. If he can pay you."

"I am nae pauper even though I am not the head of our clan." Ross looked down for a long time. "She was my only daughter. Aye, if he can find the truth of it for my poor lass, I'll pay him right enough."

Ruthven flicked a dismissive hand. "The assize will be recalled in three days then." He turned on his heel and took a step toward a door.

"Wait, my lord sheriff," the priest called out. "Bide a moment. She cannae be buried, given rites, until we are sure her death was nae self-murder. What's to be done with her body?"

The sheriff looked over his shoulder. "In this cold it will keep. Have it shoved into one of the dungeon cells until the matter is settled." He banged the door behind him with utter finality.

Patrik Ross's face was so pallid it was nearly green. He stumbled to the wall and propped himself up with a trembling hand. "Shove her into one of the dungeons..." he moaned. He grimaced and wiped his brow with the back of his hand. Turning his gaze to Law, he asked, "What am I to do?"

Law couldn't help his heavy sigh. "Who found her? I need to learn more about what happened."

Ross waved vaguely toward the door. "They sent him away when the assize was dismissed, but someone can direct you to him."

Law patted the man's shoulder sympathetically. "You bide at Blackfriars?" When Ross nodded, Law continued, "Hie yon, and I'll come speak with you." The man obviously needed time to regain his composure.

Shoulders slumped, Ross trudged away. Law waved back the guards who were about to lift the draped body upon the planks where it lay. He pulled the sheet back.

The body was discolored, mottled from having been frozen in the snow. Her mouth was open in rictus. In a scream? It might have dropped open if she had lain on her back in the snow. He needed to learn how she had lain. Her arms were cocked with her hands near her head, still stiff and unmovable when Law tried to straighten the elbow. The fingers were outstretched, claw-like. The mottling of the skin made it impossible to tell whether there were bruises, but there were no cuts to be seen.

Law shook his head. Something was odd about her appearance, but who could know what paroxysms she might have had as she died.

At Blackfriars Abbey, a wiry and grizzled friar, a plaid wrapped over his black hooded cloak as protection from the icy wind, led Law through the winter garden toward the guesthouses. They made their way round the walkway beneath high vaulting, past the refectory where the scent of beans, kale, and onions cooking for the next meal drifted, and through a narrow covered passage between the large chapter house and the chapel.

The silent friar led Law into a snow-piled courtyard that led to the guest lodgings. To the right was the ornate gleaming marble façade of the royal lodging where the king resided when he visited his favorite city. He preferred to hold his parliaments in Perth. Across the courtyard facing them was the guest hall where Law was to meet Patrik Ross, who was staying there as did many when in Perth. They passed through the snowy courtyard that held several marble benches serving to help pile up snow, a wooden shelter stacked with faggots, and a line of rose bushes bare except for jagged icicles.

"Sir Patrik should be in the last room in the corridor," the friar said. He opened the door, motioned for Law to proceed, and left, softly closing the door.

The gray daylight coming through the windows made little difference in the unlit corridor. The walls were paneled in pine, and a large crucifix and painted woodcuts of Saint

Andrew and Saint Dominic hung on the wall. At Law's knock, Sir Patrik Ross opened the door.

His sparse hair stood on end as though he'd been running his hands through it. He was ordinary, just a bland, aging man with a ruddy complexion; his clothing was of good quality, but his dark wool houppelande hung askew. Ross bowed rather stiffly and motioned for Law to enter.

The chamber was tolerably furnished with a cushioned settle, two stools at a small table, an unlit brazier, and a door leading to another room. On each side of the window hung a narrow, slightly faded tapestry. Law took a seat by the window, facing Ross.

"Do you think you can help us?" Ross asked.

Law raised an eyebrow. "Us?"

"My poor daughter and me." He shook his head. "It may be hopeless. I ken that."

"It may be hopeless, and it may not be. We will satisfy ourselves one way or the other, Sir Patrik. You said she wrote a letter."

"A cleric wrote it for her since she could nae write herself; she did nae say who." He got it out of the top of a small oaken kist sitting against the wall. "I dinnae see how you can just go around and find out things about her from people."

Law shrugged. "I'll just let people tell me about her. Most likely they'll want to talk about what happened, so it won't be as hard as you think."

The letter was written in a fine hand, and at the bottom was a clumsily written signature. It read: *I'd nae have you fash yourself, Father. I am safe and snug in Saint Leonard's Priory. The prioress has treated me most kindly, and mornings I aid the canonesses in the hospital where they serve the ill of Perth. Archibald had my clothing conveyed to me and a few coins from my dower lands' rents so I dinnae suffer want.*

But I must tell you wonderful news, Father. Maister Kennedy made my acquaintance whilst one of his students was confined at the hospital. He was most wonderful in visiting the boy, a beacon of kindness. When he heard my sad story, he vowed to aid me. He gave me his oath that he will see my case conveyed before the Holy Father. No one can deny that my grandfather was a cousin to Archibald's. The consanguinity cannae be denied. We should have never been wed.

Law asked, "This Maister Kennedy? Who is that?"

"He's the maister at the Saint John's song school. A well-respected cleric, I have heard, though I have nae met the man."

Law frowned at the letter in his hand. A cleric who barely knew her offering such aid was strange. But then he hadn't known her or the cleric, so perhaps he was wrong. "I'll need to speak to this Maister Kennedy. His offering to aid her with a divorce must have surprised you."

Ross paused. "A bit. I thought mayhap he was trying to ease her mind, just spinning a tale."

"How long ago did the letter reach you?"

"Only two weeks past. You can see that she was well. She had no reason to harm herself. She would have never run out into a storm, so someone must have forced her."

"Yet there was nae a mark on her."

"You won't help us? The lord sheriff said—"

"I shall try, but I won't lie to you. I'll find out what I can and piece together what I find into some alternatives. Then I'll check out the alternatives."

"Please. Try."

"A little more information would help. About her and this marriage she was escaping."

"She was the only child live-born with my first lady wife. That was a hard thing to have only one bairn, but we doted on her. My wife died three years ago just before Jannet married Sir Archibald Dunbar, cousin four times removed from the present Lord Dunbar." He flickered a wan smile. "I have a wee son from my new wife. Any road, Sir Archibald is well set up with a tower keep nae far from Linlithgow, so it was a good match. But her marriage did nae go well; he kept a whore and shoved it into my lass's face. Brought the woman into their very bed. If only he had been a little bit more sensible about it, kept his light wench privily as a decent man would...she would nae have taken insult and left." He shook his head dejectedly. "He could have dragged her back, and none would have telt him nae, but he thought she'd return. Mayhap she would have. In the meantime, his whore kept him well occupied, I heard tell. "

"Where is he the now? Do you ken?"

"Here in Perth. He rode here after he received word she was dead. I suppose because it would have looked ill had he not."

"Her dowry? It will be returned to you, I suppose?"

Ross frowned. "Aye. I hadn't thought of it, but of course."

"And she was staying at Saint Leonard's Priory. So some there must have kent her or at the hospital if she aided the canonesses in their work." There would be an infirmarer at Saint Leonard's Priory who would be worth speaking to as well as Sir Archibald and Maister Kennedy. "How long will you be staying in Perth?"

"Until this matter is settled. With winter upon us, my keep and lands are quiet. But I pray to the Holy Virgin this is settled quickly and the poor lass laid to rest." Running his hands through his hair, Ross sighed.

Law gave the man a direct look. "It will be. Determining whether I can find any possibility will not take so long. But important names are involved in this. Dunbar is a name not to be trifled with. The maister of the song school is an important position, a cleric the church would not give over lightly. Other names may come up as well. The lord sheriff wants it settled. You heard him say he would only give us a few days.

So don't raise your hopes too high. Even if I find something to turn over to Sir William, it still might come to nothing. It would have to be absolute proof, unless it's against someone of no importance."

Patrik Ross's face fell into the long lines of a sad hound. "So we may learn who harmed my lass and not be able to..."

"You must ken how the world works. We might have a reasonable certainty and be able to do nothing about it if we cannae convince Sir William."

"I would kill them myself!"

Law frowned thoughtfully. "Aye. You might. And find yourself in the king's dungeon. Or hanged if your lord did nae take your part. And what of your lands and people? Your wife and son?"

Ross looked down for a long time and gave a small jerky nod. When he looked up, his face was a pasty white. "Aye. You're right. I cannae throw my life away."

"I'm sorry."

"Is there any way I can help?"

"I doubt it. I would nae expect people would speak freely to you."

"Do you need to keep that?" Ross motioned to the letter Law still had beneath his hand. "I...I dinnae want anything to happen to it."

Law tapped his finger thoughtfully on the parchment. "I'll take care with it, but it's possible that it might be of use." The bells of the church began to toll sext for the midday prayers, so he rose. "I'm going to go over to Saint Leonard's Priory and see whether I can speak to the infirmarer." It would be a good place to start.

3

LOOKING FOR ANSWERS

Sister Mhairi Dorothea was a short woman of about forty, plump under her dark robe and white surplice. She was a scurrying little woman, pink of face, scrubbed and starched, with prominent blue eyes in her round face.

She strode through the white-washed hall of the hospital, past a canoness on her knees scrubbing the wood floor and simple cots where the ill lay beneath piled blankets. Out of sight, someone was moaning. She led Law into a simple office with a table stacked with lists beside an inkwell and quill. She sat behind it and motioned him to a stark wooden stool on the other side.

"Did she seem worried, Sister?"

"Worried? Sir Law, she had left her lord husband. Certes, she was worried ever since she came to stay with us, but..." She blinked her protuberant eyes several times.

"Did you ken her well? Were you fond of her? She'd been here what? Two months or thereabouts?"

"Aye, just past two months." She studied her folded hands. "It is not the place of a canoness to have particular friends, nor do I have time for gossip, if it were allowed. But she was a...a pleasant woman. Her aid in the hospital was kindly given. There was good in her in spite—" She broke off, and a blush traveled up her face to her forehead.

"I'm nae gossip, Sister. I'll repeat nothing you tell me unless it is to the lord sheriff or the lady's father because of need. They have a right to ken what happened to her. If something led up to her death, I need to hear it."

She shook her head. "I dinnae ken that it led up to it, but the time she spent with Maister Kennedy had begun to cause gossip. And in the last weeks, she spent much time away from Saint Leonard's, spent less time aiding with the sick. But she would not have confided in me, nor would I have encouraged it. So I cannae tell you more."

"But you think she was spending time with Maister Kennedy? More than you approved of as he is a priest?"

Her mouth thinned. "Aye. And she was a married woman not obeying her husband. Of course, they should not have had a particular friendship. But whether it went further than decency, I thank the Virgin Mary, I dinnae ken anything about it."

Law cleared his throat, realizing one motive for suicide. "She had been friends with Maister Kennedy for a few weeks then?" He wondered how to delicately raise the subject of a pregnancy with the canoness.

"Och. You are thinking the obvious." Her mouth twitched at his raised eyebrows. "I run a hospital for the poor, not just for our canonesses. I ken the results of a man and a woman's friendship. But I saw no signs of it in Jannet, and I think it had not been long enough that she could have been certain. Whatever I may think of her friendship with Maister Kennedy, she was nae flighty lass. She was a determined young woman. She was strong and healthy, that I can tell you from the work she did here. Maister Kennedy saw her to the door on her way home just two nights before she died, so that had nae changed. Her husband had sent her funds from her dowry, so rule out that she lacked money. Her husband..." Her mouth twisted with distaste. "...was too busy creeping after his light women to bother her, though I suppose at some time he would have demanded her back. But he seemed in nae hurry about it."

She stood, went to the window and opened the shutter to look out onto the snow-covered garden, her back to Law. "There was nothing timid about Jannet. She did nae start or flutter about over nothing. I cannae imagine her running out into the snow in a fit of melancholy." She closed the shutters with a snap and turned. "I dinnae ken what to think."

Putting a smile into his voice, Law said, "So mayhap it was murder."

"It would make more sense than self-harm."

"Would it?"

"Wait," she said with her prominent eyes glowing with indignation, "I did nae say she was murdered, just that killing herself made no sense. Not in the woman I'd seen aiding in the hospital. I did nae ken her well, but she was too steady for that."

Law stretched his legs out before himself and nodded lazily. The sister might be a hard woman—probably had to be running a hospital mainly serving the poor of the burgh of Perth—but everything about her told him she said what she believed and not what was convenient. Yes, someone like her might lie, but it would be for a motive she considered a greater good. He did not find her kindly, but he could believe her.

"Do you think an accident might be more likely than murder?"

"Certes. She might have thought she could reach shelter before the storm reached her. And who would kill Jannet? She had done none harm. She had no riches to steal or inherit. Who had reason to harm her?"

Law gave her his most innocent smile. "Oh, several people, I suspect. You because you wanted to end the scandal and feared it might touch Saint Leonard's. Maister Kennedy because she threatened his position, mayhap she threatened to go to the bishop with a story of an affair if he angered her. Her husband if he tried to force her to return and she resisted. Or someone who wanted her husband free to marry again. Or someone passing who just frightened her out into the snow."

She gave a snort that was almost a laugh. "You could be a troubadour penning romances with such fanciful tales."

"I've spent too much time catching petty thieves for merchants." His mouth twitched with a wry smile. "My mind is aflame with possibilities."

"It might be one of the other sisters offended at a married woman staying amongst us. Someone who envied her warm wool dresses and thought to gain them. Or one of Maister Kennedy's older students she refused who couldn't stand the shame of it." She snorted in amusement again.

"You could be a troubadour as well, Sister."

"Aye, but it had to be an accident. I cannae see any other cause that makes sense. Do you ken how many people die in Perth every year from the cold? Every winter we see the snow and cold and forget to fear it. Or are just too poor to have peat to burn to keep warm. The weans are the worst. Their mam thinks they're asleep, and they toddle into the storm. Just two days ago, it was a bairn not even in his second year. He was still breathing when they brought him to us, but there was naught we could do. He died without ever awakening."

"I saw Jannet's body, laid out for the inquest. It was discolored from being frozen, hard to tell whether there were marks other than that. There were none I could make out."

"Can you convince the lord sheriff it was an accident? It had to have been."

"Not without talking with more people, on your word alone. And I need to talk to whoever found her body. Forbye, I have her father insisting it had to be murder."

"Talk to more people? You mean Maister Kennedy?

"He is one of them. Did she have a chamber in the guest hall? I need to see where she stayed."

The canoness frowned at him, deep lines between her eyes, her blue stare hard and direct. "Men are not allowed to visit yon."

"It's not near the sisters' cells, is it? So there would be nae harm in it. The lord sheriff is insistent this must be solved."

The canoness let out a gust of a sigh.

Law gave her an appealing look. "I'd tell no one I was yon, but I need to see whether there is a hint in her things of what happened. If there is any way to convince the priests to give her a proper burial, for her soul if not for her father's sake, surely you'd want to do that."

"Aye. You have the right of it," she said, rubbing at the lines between her eyes as though her head ached. "The guesthouse mainly takes in women on pilgrimage, and in the winter, it was empty except for Jannet, so there is nae harm in it, it seems to me. A canoness secular can lead you yon. But be quick. We can afford nae more scandal."

She strode to the door, habit swishing around her, and called out, "Sister Beatrice."

A thin, sharp-faced canoness, hands folded into her wide sleeves, entered the doorway. Her face pinched into an expression of holy disapproval when she saw Law behind the infirmarer. "Aye, Sister? Are you all right?"

"I need you to show Sir Law to Jannet's chamber. Wait while he looks about, and then see him on his way." She gave Law a cool and pointed glance.

Sister Beatrice sniffed with disapproval but bowed her head in obedience. She motioned for Law to follow her through the bare, whitewashed hallway, walls lined with wooden crucifixes of a writhing, suffering Christ, into the guest hall.

With a droll smile of thanks, Law closed the door in her face and stood alone in the chamber. The air was icy, the small brazier in a corner unlit, but a hint of rose attar was still in the air. It was a bare room, with a few pegs on the wall—one holding a green kirtle heavily embroidered around the hem—a narrow bed, and a wooden kist against a wall opposite the only window. He opened the shutters to let in the watery winter light and began his search with the kist. It was filled with good woolen clothes suitable for the winter though some were well-worn, a plaid that she must have used as a wrap, and a small wooden casket. He dumped the contents onto the bed: a piece of Cairngorm crystal, rough and unpolished, a tied bundle of dried flowers, and a small seashell with purple stripes. Keepsakes, of what he could not tell. He dropped them back in, shoved the clothes into place, and looked around. He pulled back the coverlets on the narrow bed. Nothing but a plain linen coverlet. There was a little dust beneath the bed and no place left to search.

When he left, Sister Beatrice was waiting, her mouth pursed up with displeasure. "It took you long enough. Did you find what you were seeking?"

"Aye. Thank you."

She gave a decisive turn to lead him out and said over her shoulder, "A priest spending time with a married woman. A scandal."

"True enough, Sister."

"I cannae count the times she came in as the doors were locked. Twice she did nae return at all and sent a message she had tarried with a friend. Mayhap she was with him every time. Mayhap not. Even worst was him prancing after a skirt like a fool, and him in charge of the song school to lead lads astray."

"Has anyone else been in her chamber since it happened?"

"The guest hall is empty the now. But I have better things to do than keep track of people's comings and goings."

"Did you see her at all that day?"

"Two days ago, aye. From afar. I saw her come walking back from the hospital when the bells were ringing Terce for midmorning prayers, then scurrying out the door not long after prayers were done."

Cormac was quiet as he shoved the door shut behind him with a foot, his arms filled with two loaves of bread and a pitcher of ale. Looking up from slicing a dish of potted herring on the table, Law thought Cormac looked grim and thoughtful, his mouth in a thin line.

"Snowing again?"

"Nae. An icy wind though." Cormac shrugged. "You would nae think it would bother me. 'Tis years since but it brought it all back. My siuir, the youngest, she had eight years, old enough to ken better than to go out into a storm. I think she wanted to check on the cats in the byre. We were never sure..."

Law put down the knife. "I did nae ken."

"We were doing one thing or another. None of us saw her slip out. She must have been confused in the snow." Cormac blinked hard. "It took three days to find her body." He thumped the pitcher onto the table harder than necessary. "Och, there is nae point thinking on something that cannae be mended and is long past." He peered suspiciously into one of the two wooden cups on the table, wiped them out with a corner of his cloak, and poured out the ale.

"Things come back to us. That happens."

"Aye, so they do. Have you lost anyone that close to you, Law?"

Law snorted. "I've made a calling of it. My parents died of the plague when I was a page in the earl's household. My older brother as well. He was my hero, the best on a horse or in the practice yard. I spent much of my life trying to be as good as he was, until I realized it was nothing but childish hero-worship. But still if I ever do anything right, there's this glimmer in my mind that says, 'Look at this, David.' And then I feel the loss. He was one of the deftest men I ever saw with a sword. I guess sometimes I still try to live up to his approval. And I lost my comrade-in-arms—not family but as close. Mayhap closer. We fought together. Shared tents on the march. Drank and argued and—" Law shook his head. "He was more than a brother. He died beside me at Verneuil. That I saved myself but not him—" Law swallowed hard. "Sometimes I think I see him on the street and then realize it's just a trick of my eyes."

Cormac smiled wistfully. "Are you trying to make me feel better? I dinnae think it's working."

Law breathed a chuckle through his nose. "Probably not."

Cormac slid a cup of ale toward him. After a drink, Law spread potted herring thickly onto a piece of bread for the minstrel.

Cormac sat on a stool and stretched out his rangy legs in an indolent pose. In the dim light of the candlelit room, he squinted thoughtfully ahead. His hair was a glossy red, his eyes clear blue, his face a long oval, a bit bony. Law thought Cormac handsome in his own way, though not showy in spite of the red stripes of his doublet. At last the minstrel swallowed the last bite of his bread and asked, "What about this dead woman, Jannet? It must have been an accident. She probably lost herself in the snow. 'Tis easy enough to do as I ken all too well."

"Possibly, but what was she doing so far from Saint Leonard's? Was she yon to talk to someone? Who? Why was she alone? Some questions may be answered when I talk to the man who found her body. But aye, there are questions. Her father had that much of the right of it."

"That is a long way from home. But she still could have been lost in the snowstorm."

"It is too distant to believe that she just wandered yon. No, there must have been a reason she was so far from home. I'll have to see what people say. And whether they tell the same tale. I'm curious to see what Maister Kennedy has to say about all this aid he was supposedly giving her."

"I can help. Give me something to do."

"I'll think of something," Law lied.

"Don't spin me a tale." Cormac glowered. "I helped you before, you ken."

Law sighed. He could only hope this wouldn't be as dangerous as the last time Cormac had helped him. "I will think of something. I just haven't found out enough yet."

After he was stretched out on his cot, Law reread the letter that some cleric, mayhap even Kennedy, had written for Jannet to send to her father.

He was most wonderful in visiting the boy—a beacon of kindness. When he heard my sad story, he vowed to aid me. He gave me his oath...

After he snuffed the candle, he kept thinking back to what she said Kennedy had offered. He wondered about Kennedy. At the least, it was a most peculiar thing for a cleric to do. First, he had to find out from Kennedy whether the story was the truth. If it was, why, by all the Saints, would he would have gone to such expense and risked a great scandal?

Where would he have found the money for such an expensive undertaking? Certainly, no one would believe the story that it was done innocently.

Jannet was spinning in a snowstorm, like a leaf, wearing her green embroidered kirtle, her long hair blowing wide. She kept whirling, her mouth agape with a voiceless scream. Then the dead earl of Douglas's voice boomed, "You failed her, Law. You failed me and let me die. You failed your friend, Iain. You never do anything right."

Law ran up narrow tower stairs. He had to find his dead lord and make him stop before everyone knew how much Law had failed him. But when he reached the top of the stairs, gasping for breath, Sister Mhairi Dorothea was bending over a body on a bed. The body was Jannet. Ice encased her face, and her open mouth was stuffed with snow. The sister was cutting away Jannet's clothing with a gleaming knife. She frowned at Law. "Open the window. She must go back into the storm."

Law awoke in the dark, sat straight up, gasping for breath. He sat on the edge of the bed and ran hands through sweat-dampened hair. The wind rattled the shutters like the clatter of bones. It made him feel as though the room were a crypt.

❧

"D*eum verum, unum in Trinitáte, et Trinitátem in Unitáte, veníte, adorémus.*"

Crystalline boys' voices filled the air as Law hammered with the iron knocker. A stooped, hollow-eyed friar opened the door. When Law said he was here to see Maister Kennedy, he said, "The maister is out the now." But Law insisted, so he led Law down the hall. "I'm Brother Nevan, the doorkeeper. Yon is Brother Hugh's office, the maister's assistant."

When Law opened the door, Brother Hugh looked up

with one blond eyebrow raised in inquiry. Law smiled and explained that he had questions authorized by the lord sheriff for the song school maister.

"I dinnae ken when Maister Kennedy will be here. He has sent no message."

Law waited as a reedy young student was sent to relay instructions to someone named Brother David. An older priest left with an armful of parchments. Then, for the first time, Law was alone with the most striking man he had ever seen, even in the stark black of a friar's robes. He was taller even than Law, broad-shouldered. He sat straight on his stool writing at top speed some lengthy list. When he rose to cross the room for a document from a side table, he moved smoothly with athletic self-possession. His dark gold hair was in lively curls around a small tonsure and bounced as he nodded to himself as he worked. He was in his early twenties, Law guessed. Brother Hugh sanded the list he had been working on and put it on a third table with several others.

"I suppose the song school must be complicated to run," Law said.

"We have a great many matters to keep straight," Brother Hugh said, smiling. "Managing the lands that support the school, contributions, and keeping discipline with the students... But this is a slow time with the foul weather. A good time to catch up with things. Many of the students have returned home for a time, and we aren't preparing for a major feast. I prefer it when things are frantic and bustling. God wants us to keep our hands busy."

"Is Maister Kennedy also having a slow time?"

From the hardening of the friar's expression, Law knew he had made a misstep, although he wasn't sure how.

"As I telt you an hour ago, Sir Law, I am the maister's assistant. If you tell me what you need from Maister Kennedy, mayhap I can save you some time. The school has no connection to the lord sheriff, so why would he send you here? "

"This is just a routine burgh matter that Sir William asked me to take care of for him."

Brother Hugh went back to sit on the corner of his table, folded broad hands at his waist, and frowned at Law. "If it is a routine burgh matter, then I should be able to take care of it, and you need nae bother him with it."

"His involvement in it...his being a priest and his involvement in it, I think he would prefer that it be discussed privily."

Hugh's eyes widened, and he pursed his lips. "It would nae have to do with Jannet Neyn Patrik Ross, would it?"

Law raised his eyebrows in false surprise. "It is delicate."

"I heard students gossiping, saying she had died. He will nae take well to you bothering him about her."

"If he refuses to aid me, all I can do is inform the lord sheriff. Whether Sir William will take it to the lord bishop I cannae say."

"So it is about her."

Law shrugged.

"Then you will have to speak to Maister Kennedy. I ken nothing about the woman. I did nae want to." His expression had tightened. He sat behind his table and spread a fresh piece of parchment, then plunged his quill into the inkwell as though to stab it.

"Have you been a friar long?"

"Five years."

That did not surprise Law. Like many, the friar must have been sent young to a monastery. Casually, Law said, "I suppose it is natural you'd be angry she took up so much of Maister Kennedy's time."

Brother Hugh laid his quill down and looked at Law with a puzzled expression. "Why would I be angry? It is a woman's way to try to tempt men from saintliness, but the maister is a good priest. I feel sorrow and pity that it is so, but woman brought the stench of evil upon herself in the Garden of Eden. It is nae for me to question. I won't think upon women enticing men into their evil ways, intoxicating them with the sins of the flesh. I don't ken about such things or want to. I'm sorry she died without a priest yon to give her unction and forgive her for her sins. But men are safe from her enticements, and that must have been God's will. God's will is my will. I have no will of my own." His voice had taken on the rhythm of a street friar preaching damnation. He gave a small shake, smiled, and said in a normal tone, "I have no reason to be angry."

Law kept his tone casual. "Of course, I understand about temptation." Aye, Law did, but he'd certainly share nothing about that with this friar.

"I suppose that you do. Most men feel it, I am telt, but evil cannae touch me. It was God's will that I be given a face and shape that draws women to me with their soft touches and sleekit ways. He made me desirable to the daughters of Eve to test me. My father wanted me to marry, and the woman was fair to look upon. She brushed her hands against me, tried to entice me with sweet scents and soft smiles. I spent a week on my knees begging Christ to deliver me from any uncleanness. He told me to withdraw from the world and spurn all such filth." Again he dropped his preaching tone for a normal one. "I suppose most men know about temptation."

"And Maister Kennedy is free from temptation as well?"

Brother Hugh scowled at Law. "That you must ask him about. He is a priest and should be above such things, but..." He shook his head. "I wish I kent where he is today. It is odd that he is nae here, so I can make you no promises that you can speak to him."

Law stood. "Suppose I come back later to see whether he's here then."

"I am fasting today and shall be here all the day, so I can finish my work. Would you like me to tell him you were seeking him?"

Law grinned. "You will any road."

"Aye." Brother Hugh had a bright-eyed smile. "But I wondered what you would say."

Law shook his head. "I'm sure you'll do whatever you think is right."

The snow had hardened to a thick layer of ice on North Street. Law passed through North Port, its heavy gates open and a guard huddling in the protection of the guardhouse door. Then he followed the track that led by the wide, ice-covered Town Ditch dug to protect the burgh in one of the wars with the English.

It was a typical suburb. A saddler's yard with harnesses hanging from the eves of sturdy stone house, was cheek to jowl by a dyer where apprentices stirred steaming vats of dye in a neatly shoveled yard. An ice-slick path ran between the two. The path wended its way past a mix of hovels and decent stone houses, shutters closed against the biting wind. Usually there would have been carts lurching past, but the snow was still too deep for traffic. The high walls of Blackfriars Abbey rose in the distance, past a field of deep drifts sculpted into mounds around bushes and trees.

The house Law sought was in the middle of the suburb farther from the port than he had thought, judging by the stench of curing hides. A dog took up barking as he stepped through the gate.

"Maister!" A lad in a tattered tunic stopped shoveling snow to shout and point toward Law.

The yard was busy in spite of the snow, with the lad shoveling and a journeyman stirring a steaming vat that reeked strongly enough to sting Law's eyes. The master tanner was a short, sturdy, fair-haired man who frowned as he supervised the workers, his hands on his hips. He yelled for the hound to be quiet.

"I need a word with Maister Braidlaw," Law said.

The maister strode decisively toward him. "A word is it, sir?" The man's sharp eyes assessed him, taking in his muddy boots but pausing for a moment on Law's gold spurs. "Is it about the woman Gil found the day before yesterday?" At Law's nod he continued. "Come inside the counting house and warm yourself, if you will."

"Were you with Gil when he found her?" Law asked as he followed the man into a little hut at the far end of the yard. There was a table stacked with papers against one wall, a couple of shelves on another, and scraps of leather scattered hither and yon. A small brazier cut some of the chill, and Law held out his hands to warm them.

"Right before, and if you're thinking he had anything to do with the woman, put it out of your head. He's my apprentice and sleeps on a pallet in the hut with Davey, my journeyman." He sat on a stool and gestured to another. He leaned forward, elbows on the table, pushing aside a docket of papers. "With finished hides on the premises, even after a storm I take care about thieves. The dog was raising a fuss like, so I kent there was something amiss. I sent Gil out with it on a lead to find out what had the animal in a lather." He grimaced with distaste. "He came running back without even the dog, screaming like a lassie. Had to send Davey to find the animal, but the dog was with the...the body. Standing guard, Davey said. I sent Davey for the watch for I could nae send Gil, he was shaking and huddling in his pallet like a wean. Though I cannae say I blame him that much."

"Did you see the body yourself?"

"Aye, certes. I went to stand guard over it while Davey was away."

"Had the body been moved? After Gil found it, I mean"

Maister Braidlaw scowled. "I dinnae think so. Gil had brushed away the snow, or tried to. She was all stiff like, as a body would be after a while."

"I'll need to talk to him, to find out how she lay when he found her."

"You have my permission. He's a good enough lad, a mite lazy at times, but honest withal."

Leaving Maister Braidlaw shuffling papers, Law paused in the doorway. Gil was speaking intently to the journeyman who still stirred the steaming vat. The stench was even stronger, and Law's eyes watered. He was eager to be away, so he motioned to the lad.

As Gil approached, a bit timidly, Law said, "Your maister said you could tell me about the morning you found the lady in the snow." He thrust his chin toward the gate. "Come walk with me whilst we talk."

Gil wrinkled his brow and looked toward the doorway of the counting house, but Maister Braidlaw stepped into view and nodded to him. The lad said, "Och, there's nae much to tell."

Outside the gate after a deep breath of somewhat fresher air, Law continued, "Maister Braidlaw said the dog was raising a fuss."

"Aye, he had been for a good while. When I took him through the gate, he headed straight for where she lay. Near pulled my arm out, he was lunging so."

Out on the track that ran toward the Ditch and the city wall beyond, he looked around again. There were six houses which ran down to the Ditch, several with kale yards within their fences. Peat smoke drifted above the roofs of all except one close by. Farther from the Ditch was a dyer's yard. Breathing in air with less stink, Law kept walking as he asked, "How did she lay? She was covered with snow?"

"I could see a bit of her blue cloak. Angus dug at the snow that was covering her until I shoved him back and brushed her off some..." The boy gulped, paling at the memory. "She was facedown, but I had no thought she was dead. I took her hand thinking...though it sounds daft...to pull her up. But it was...stiff. Her fingers like sticks. And cold as ice."

So even then she'd been dead long enough to have stiffened when Gil found her. After battles, he'd seen bodies stiffen in as little as three or four hours, though when it was cold, stiffening seemed to take longer. At any rate, she'd been dead a good time.

"Can you pick out exactly where you found her?"

Gil pointed across the track from his master's yard to a much-trampled spot. The storm had howled like a bean sìth. Had Jannet cried for help, no one would have heard—except perhaps the good hound.

"So she was stiff and icy cold. How was her body? You say she lay face down? Mayhap curled up for warmth?"

"No," he said uncomfortably. "Her legs were stretched out straight, like, with her hands..." He raised his arms even with his head. "Like so. They were shoved deep into the snow as though she tried to push herself up."

"As though she had fallen?" Law asked in a casual tone.

The lad tilted his head as he stared hard at the spot. "Thinking back on it, her clothes when the dog was at the snow, her skirts were smoothed over her legs. Not hiked about as you'd expect if she'd fallen and struggled to get up."

Law nodded at the comment and looked about. Where she'd been found was a level spot where no drifts would have formed. The snow was up to his knees in a fairly even covering, except where it was trampled into the dirt. The snow other than that showed no helpful sign at all, not surprising. Had there been any footprints, they would have been covered in the course of the storm. He stood looking at the glimmering snow, a raven cawing from a snow heaped hawthorn, and the houses with gardens that sloped down to the Ditch. The occupants of those houses would have to be spoken to.

"I need to finish my work or the maister will make me work late the eve," Gil said, shifting his feet.

"Aye." Law realized that Terce was ringing at Blackfriars. Winter dark fell early. He had best hurry to speak to one more suspect, so he slipped the boy a coin and dismissed him. It had been a long day, and he wanted ale and a warm fire to thaw his icy-cold feet from the trudge through the snow. Worse, after the laborious walk, a fiery throb was lancing his scarred leg, but he wrapped his cloak close as he walked back through the city gates and across the burgh.

The streets within the gates had cleared enough that the city was once again beginning to move. A woman passed carrying a load of peat on her back; folks left the market with goods they had bought. A troop of mounted men splashed through the slush, the crowned heart of the Douglas clan on their cloaks.

The sky was already turning to slate gray with livid rosy streaks in the west. Blowing eddies of snow blurred the buildings as he passed. He stepped into the rutted stable yard at the house on Watergate Street. The house, screened from the street by ice-draped trees, had seen better days. It must have once been imposing, but several shutters now hung askew, and lichen streaked the walls. A horse snorted within the ramshackle stable.

He gritted his teeth and climbed the steps to the doorway, the throbbing in his leg growing worse at every step. As he reached the top step, Archibald Dunbar—in a shiny dark blue doublet unfastened at the neck and hose—opened the door and said, "Stop right there. What do you want?"

Dunbar's face was weathered; he had heavy shoulders and a ham-like hand clenched into a fist. His hair was blond and his lashes and brows so light they could barely be seen. His pudgy face was twisted into a snarl. He might have been intimidating except for the paunch beneath the loosened doublet and the blood-red veins in his eyes.

"I need to speak to you about your wife's death."

"What about it? What business is it of yours?"

"I have some questions—"

Dunbar snarled. "Get out."

"I won't take much of your time, but—"

"You won't take any of it. I'll nae answer any questions about Jannet. So go on back out of my yard."

Law almost smiled to himself. Traveling with an army, you learned to handle this kind of bully. He stepped close to Dunbar and glared into his eyes. "You daft bastard. Is that the message you want me to take back to the lord sheriff then, that you refuse to help with the assize? He sent me to see that this is settled as quickly and quietly as possible. And if you think you can push me about, I'll soon show you differently." He took another step in through the doorway as Dunbar backed away.

"Why did you nae say that the lord sheriff sent you?"

"I just did."

"You have no idea the priests and messengers coming to my door, bothering me..." His scowl altered to a look of petulant self-pity. "But whatever they say, Jannet did nae harm herself. And no one shall blame me for driving her to it."

"The lord sheriff tasked me to ascertain what happened before he reconvenes the assize. Now if you will spare me a wee bit of your time, Sir Archibald..."

"Aye. Come along to the fire where it is warm. There is mulled wine, and we'll talk. I did nae mean to go at you like that. It's been hard, you see, what with this and that."

"It is painful, of course," Law said and offered his hand. Dunbar's hand was slick with sweat, and Law quickly dropped it. He followed Dunbar into the musty-smelling room and took a cup of the warm mulled wine. It was a long, dark hall with only two chairs and a bench beside a scarred trestle table in front of the fireplace.

"Now what is this about Jannet?" Dunbar demanded as he hunched over his cup. "It's nonsense. She must have been lost in the storm. Why she'd wander about in a storm I'll never understand. Who says anything else? Why have they put off the assize?"

"She was on the opposite side of Perth from Saint Leonard's, outwith the walls, when she died. It seems strange she could have wandered so far, but for now I am just talking to people to find out what might have happened."

Dunbar shook his head, shrugged, and took a long drink of his wine.

"So she left you, and you agreed to let her go?"

"A bit more than two months ago, aye."

"She was going to seek a divorce on grounds of consanguinity, I'm telt."

"Now bide a bit. It would have taken more gold than she or her father had to take that to Rome. No, that was nae going to happen."

"You think she was going to come to her senses and return to you?"

"I hoped so. Dragging her back where she'd scream and wail until I beat her bloody was no way to live. So I was giving her time. But she would have been back eventually."

Law nodded encouragingly.

"I...I suppose I could have taken her feelings more into

account. So I had other women? A man does. Of course, I did, but I suppose I could have kept it where she did nae see. But she made this commotion about it, too. It is nae as though I kept the woman. It was just a whore, nothing to interfere with her. It was...just...one of those things a man does. A whore is nae important, after all. So I decided to give her some time."

"But you were planning to take her back."

"Certes, I was. I need an heir and a mistress for my house. " He looked around the bare room. "My house here and in Lanark needs a mistress's hand while I'm about my business with the royal court."

"She had been spending a great deal of time with Maister Kennedy. Some say he was going to help her with the divorce."

Dunbar drew back as though he'd been slapped. "How dare you spread that rumor about? There is no reason to think such a thing."

"She wrote a letter to her father and telt him so."

"She telt him what? What did she say in it?"

Law took the letter out of the breast of his doublet. "Just that he had been most particularly kind to her and would help her take the case to Rome."

Dunbar bent over the letter, moving his lips as he read. "I...I find it hard to take in. She was always so careful of what anyone would say of her. But others brought me the tittle-tattle. You're nae the first. But to invite such scandal? With a priest?"

Law took back the letter. "When did you first hear rumors?"

"Not until I returned to Perth."

"Mayhap she wanted to return and thought the scandal would keep you from agreeing. And then out of shame, she killed herself."

"To burn in Hell's fire? She would nae. And she kent I would take her back. Certes, I would have. I need a wife and an heir." His face twisted into a scowl again. "Now the whole matter of a marriage has to be thought through, and if people blame me, it will cost to make a father agree. My cousin the earl will nae be pleased. Indeed he will nae."

"Killing herself by running out into a storm, surely she would have to be crazed to do such a thing. Was she ever crazed? Did she act the madwoman?"

"Jannet? She was furious when I brought the whore into our bed, but...more cold than a madwoman. Her anger could be icy. By all the Saints, Sir Law, I cannae see Jannet harming herself at all and not that way. Freezing to death? That must be a terrible way to die."

"Then it would be more likely that it was an accident. She was lost in the snow. It can happen."

"Aye," the man said eagerly.

"But she died all the way across Perth from Saint Leonard, so how did she go so far? And why? If I cannae explain that to the lord sheriff, he won't believe the story it was an accident. That is what made them think she did it deliberately. And where she died there were houses nearby. Even in the storm, she probably would have been able to reach one."

"Mayhap she was seeking someone. There are craftsmen out that way, so that must be it. But how the devil are you ever going to find out?"

"You saw the letter she had written to her father." Law tucked it away. "If she wrote to you, telt you why she might harm herself, it would save a great deal of scandal."

Dunbar looked startled and snorted. "I look bad any road, and there is scandal no matter how it falls out." He seemed to ponder Law for a moment and sighed. "What a to-do it all is and all for a woman." "You'll find another wife, scandal or no," Law said.

"Aye. But if they noise about that I drove her to kill herself, the King will nae like it." He looked into his cup morosely before filling it again. "He dotes on the Queen, you ken. But I dinnae see why one woman is different from another."

There was the sound of hoof beats and neighing outside. Dunbar jumped to his feet, looking happy to escape his thoughts, and strode toward the door. Law followed more slowly, limping a bit. A gingery, trim man sat astride a fine chestnut palfrey a few strides from the steps. He looked down at them.

"Time to stop sulking about, Archie. Festivities are what you need. I'll drag James and Duncan back with me. And some female company as well, so be ready. In two hours, mind." His lip twisted in a leer. "Your friend can stay if you like."

"His business is done here," Archibald Dunbar said without bothering with an introduction.

The man waved his hand and turned his horse to canter out of the yard.

As he watched his friend leave, Dunbar muttered, "He never liked Jannet."

"Why?"

"Said she was against him and wanted to tame me like a pet hound." He absently scratched his stubbled cheek. "There's no more I can tell you. Now I have to have my steward find something in this hole to drink." He turned his back and trudged toward the door.

"Where were you the night before last?" Law asked.

Duncan paused but didn't turn back around. "If you think I harmed her, you're wrong. I was in Stirling. Aye, 'tis not a long ride, but I had company the night. And if she was nae at Saint Leonard's, how could I have kent where she was?" He continued into the house and let the door slam behind him.

There were ways Dunbar might have known where Jannet was, perhaps having arranged a meeting with her.

Law rubbed his chin, thinking over Dunbar's story. Finding some particular whore in Stirling would be hard unless... If she was a favorite of Dunbar or of his friends, she might be nearer than that. In spite of the near invitation, clearly Law was not welcome for their revelry. A minstrel, however, might be.

Maister Kennedy was one of those priests, and Law had met a number of them, who would have suited armor more than the black cassock he wore. He was a tall, lean, pale-eyed man with an effortless look of strength, probably some family's younger son who had been disposed of into the church. Law wondered whether he was as unsuited to it as he looked.

"Sit," Kennedy said. He went to a sideboard against an oak linenfold wall. "Join me in a glass of wine, Sir Law."

Law went through his story of being ordered by the lord sheriff to investigate Jannet's death.

"Och, so you are to rule out suicide."

"Or establish it."

Kennedy raised his eyebrow. "Why come to me?"

"It's common gossip that you were a close friend of the lady and that you were helping to send the case of her marriage to Rome."

The priest leaned back and considered Law. "Once, soon after I was first ordained, John de Lindsay—rightful Bishop of Glasgow, you ken, though still disputing it with the pope—was to celebrate the Mass here in Perth and commanded the best boys' choir. Maister Riddoch was the song maister at the time and would have the honor to train the boys' choir. But it was a chance for me, one hard to come by, to show what I could do. He had a cousin in Edinburgh whom he had had offended over a posting of a canon. The man offered to help me by sending a letter that Maister Riddoch's mother was failing, about to die, in order to lure him away and thus do Riddoch a bad turn in return. It would have given me the honor as his assistant of leading the choir before the bishop. My rise in the church would have been guaranteed for I am a better song maister than Riddoch ever thought of being." He handed a filled goblet to Law and sat behind his desk. "I dinnae do business so, Sir Law. I am an honest man."

"So you are saying...?"

"That I have nothing to hide, so ask your questions."

"I must prove what happened."

"And to prove a thing like that you have to ask private questions of everyone who kent her, I suppose. It would nae look good to the lord sheriff if someone refused."

"Probably not."

"Mayhap I should send a brother to Sir William to tell him how well you are doing in your work for him. He'd want to hear about that."

"Kind of you to mention. I'm sure that he would."

"By the Saints, you did nae even twitch. I see sleekit students every day, but none could match you."

Law raised his eyebrow. "I beg your pardon?"

"Och, give over. The lord sheriff would nae bring someone in to go about asking awkward questions, nor send you to me, a priest. So who is really paying you? Someone with a grudge against me?"

Law studied the song maister a silent moment and then said, "It is no great secret. Her father is paying me, but I was not lying. The lord sheriff agreed to it and is holding off the assize while I try to find out what happened."

Kennedy gave a small nod. "I heard that he put it off but

had nae heard why. Nor did I want to cause gossip by inquiring."

"So the story that you were good friends is true. That you were helping her with the dissolution of the marriage?"

"She had been forced into a marriage against the laws of the church. I was in a position to have the papers drawn up that she could send to the Holy See." Kennedy sighed. "In a way, I blame myself for her death. The papers were at a little house I inherited near the Northgate Port. I gave her the key and told her she could retrieve them to be sent to the Curia. I had no idea she would go when there were such signs of a storm, but... Still I blame myself. I dinnae ken why she would have done something so foolhardy."

"So that is why she was outwith the gates. Do you think it possible someone lured her away from the house? Would anyone have reason to do that?"

Kennedy's heavy face was still and grim. "I dinnae ken any reason why someone would hurt the poor lady. She was gentle. Kind. Whether she was at my house, I dinnae ken. I have nae been there since the storm. If she had the papers, that would tell."

"I'll need to check your house to see if there is any sign of her being there."

Kennedy frowned. "She had the key, so you'll need to ask the lord sheriff or his men about that."

"You could nae just give the papers to her?"

"We agreed it was best to avoid more gossip. The canonesses at Saint Leonard's were already gossiping enough."

There were several obvious gaps in the song maister's story. A big one was that nothing had been said about a key found on Jannet's body. Checking on that would be his first target. "Her father is convinced someone killed her. He says she would have never wandered out into a storm or tried to kill herself that way."

"Why would anyone kill her? There was nothing to gain by it. And luring someone out into a storm is an unlikely way to kill, any road. Of course, you could be thinking she was my light woman. You could be thinking mayhap I wanted to break it off with her, and she says she'll go to the bishop or even the King, and I have no other way to stop her."

"Aye. I thought of that."

"You'd be stupid if you didn't. Or that she was through with me, and I couldn't stand the thought of her going back to her husband. What do you think about that?"

Law twitched a smile. "You were at the song school that day until after the storm was raging. You supervised the older boys in a chorus and met with a father whose son..." Law chuckled. "I did nae hear exactly what his infraction was, but he was thrashed from what I was telt."

"Jannet's father is receiving his money's worth. But I could have paid someone to do it."

"In that case, I suspect they'd nae have chosen a snowstorm for doing it. Forbye, I dinnae think you'd give someone that much to use against you. If it was murder... I never heard of murder done so. Mayhap an impulse or chance, not meant to lead to her death."

"What about the husband? Being free to find a more agreeable wife would likely suit him well."

"Possibly. I have to confirm where he was that night. But you definitely gave her a key to your house?"

"Aye."

There was a tap at the door and Brother Hugh opened it. "Do you need me further, Maister Kennedy? 'Tis near Vespers."

"It has gone dark already, Hugh. You've done enough for the day."

"I'll prepare my mind for prayers then. I have time. You

will want to look over these for the morrow." He put a thin stack of papers in front of Kennedy.

"I shall go over them when I have time."

The friar glanced uneasily at Law. He folded his hands in his sleeves and walked out, silent except for the swish of his robes and the click of the door, and leaving a faint whiff of incense from his robes in the chill air.

After a moment of silence, Law said, "I have no more questions for now, and I have taken enough of your time."

The remnants of daylight had faded to slate gray, and the office was in darkness. Only a lurid splash of gold lit the edge of the sky. Kennedy stood and looked out the window, a dark shape in the growing murk. "'Tis grown chill," he said.

"Are we going to have more snow?" Law wondered.

"It will be a cold night."

Gusts of whirling snow flapped Law's cloak as he walked. It howled between the narrow, two-story shops and houses, scouring away the stink of piss and sweat that was a constant fug in any city. Law walked slowly to Wulle Cullen's inn.

He was glad to arrive at the warmth and a cozy smell of ale and peat fire. He sat in a corner as patrons came and went. The thick ale Wulle brought him had a bitter herbal taste, its rich malt taste filling his mouth, but he found himself staring into its depths trying to unpick the snarls of this new mess he was entangled in.

When Law made his suggestion to Cormac, the minstrel grinned and hurried to his cubby in the back to find an instrument he said would better suit his task. He gave an airy wave on his way out the door. Without Cormac's music to soothe him, Law's musings were dark indeed.

"Sir Law," a man's voice called.

When Law looked up, Patrik Ross was making his way past the trestle tables where patrons bent over horn cups of ale. Ross's clothing was straightened and neater than the last time Law spoke with him, but his face was even gaunter and more deeply lined. Law motioned to Wulle to bring them more ale. He knew he probably should have gone to speak to the man earlier, but there had hardly been a chance.

Ross dropped onto the stool opposite Law's and ran his hands through his sparse brown hair. "Have you learnt anything?"

Law held up a hand to quiet him while Wulle set a pitcher and cup on the table. When the innkeeper walked away, he poured Ross a cup. The man grasped it like a lifeline.

Law took a deep breath for a difficult talk. "Nae all there is to learn. But I do ken why she was at Northgate Port that night, so I believe we can convince the assize she did nae harm herself. She can be put to rest by the priests without that shame."

"Why?" Ross leaned toward Law. "Why was she there?"

Law took a gulp of his ale. "Kennedy sent her yon. He said it was to find papers he had left at his house regarding dissolving the marriage."

Ross's forehead creased into a deep frown. "He sent her into a storm?" The man's face reddened, and he gripped his cup so hard his fingers were white. "He... He sent her..."

Law squeezed the man's arm lightly. The muscles of Ross's arm were like tight-strung cable. "It was before the storm hit, and he said he had no idea she would go in ill weather."

Ross looked down at the cup he was still gripping as though he had never seen such a thing before. "Why would he nae just give the papers to her? That cannae be right."

Law let out a sigh. "There was talk. Gossip. About his

spending so much time with a woman who had left her husband."

The red drained from Ross's face, leaving it whey white. "That she was his leman. He had taken her as his leman."

"Gossip said so. He said it was false, so he was avoiding being seen in her company, and he sent her to find the papers." Law kept his gaze on his cup as he took a drink. "So he said."

"How could he? He a priest and she a married woman. A good lass in spite of it all." Ross pushed himself to his feet. "How could he?"

Law rose and put a firm hand on the man's shoulder. "It's over. The poor lass is dead, but at least there will be a decent burial. See to prayers for her soul, and let all this go, man."

Ross shook his hand off and stumbled toward the door.

4

Cormac observed that Sir Archibald Dunbar was clearly at home. There was light in the windows, and the shutters, though askew, were open. Voices and laughter of both men and women floated into the evening. He followed the sound, climbed the ice-slick stone steps, and knocked loudly on the door, lute under his arm.

The door was opened by a man with a curly mop of gingery hair, a livid yellow doublet, and a beaker of wine in his hand. "Archie," he called over his shoulder, "did you hire a minstrel?"

Cormac shook his head with a smile. "He did nae hire me, but I heard you might be in need of music, so I came."

"A minstrel? Then let him in, Andrew." A woman came forward in well-worn finery, threadbare velvet, and long, dark hair loose onto her shoulders.

"Aye," said the man who had answered the door. He gave Cormac a speculative look. "Come in if you have a braw tune."

There were a dozen people in the room and a large fire blazing on the hearth. In the middle of the room was a trestle table piled with a platter of sausages scented with onion and sage, loaves of bread, and more flagons of wine than Cormac could count. A dozen torches in wall sconces gave the night a flickering glow. The seating were stools and only two chairs. He could identify Archibald Dunbar, slumped in one of the chairs with a beaker of wine in his hand, from Law's description.

"Play!" the woman who had insisted he be invited in commanded. She plopped down on Dunbar's knee and slid her arm around his neck. He seemed to pay her no mind as he drained his wine cup.

Cormac unwound the protective cloth from his lute and quickly plucked the strings to check that it was still in tune. The lute had never been his best instrument, but it would allow him to move about the room to listen. He struck up the notes of "I Long for Thy Virginitie" as he strolled about the room, smiling and nodding to the men and women as he passed. The song no doubt would suit the company.

The party began sedately enough, with the men more interested in the platter of food than the women clinging to their arms. Soon their attention turned to emptying the flagons of wine. Then there were squeals of laughter. Bodices were loosened, one of the men pushed playfully away after slapping a rear. Dunbar was sullenly drinking, though, which seemed to put a bit of a damper on the mood.

One by one, Cormac paused by the men, but there was no conversation to listen to, just drunken jests and boasting of prowess at on the field or in bed. None of it would help. Were they drunk enough to forget he was only a minstrel if he asked where they had been the night Jannet died?

Just as Cormac was convinced he would learn nothing, the wind came whirling upon them. A couple of shutters thudded open and banged against the wall. The torches sputtered and gutted. The woman on Dunbar's knee gave a shriek. Several of the men dashed to grab the shutters and wrestle them closed. Cormac paused in his playing, but it appeared that the interruption would not end the festivities. Beneath the whistling of the wind, he sensed a lusty excitement. Soon, in the semidarkness broken only by the blaze in the fireplace, he heard laughing, a squeal of false protest, a rip of material. First one pair and then another disappeared into the murk toward other chambers.

When Cormac decided to give up on the entire endeavor and make for the door, unpaid in money or information, he caught his foot on a fallen stool in the darkness and stumbled several steps, clutching his lute to his chest, until someone caught him imperiously by the arm and pulled him upright.

The man put a hand on Cormac's shoulder and said, "Careful of the hazards of the night, my lad." There was enough light to make out the man with a curly mop of ginger hair who had opened the door, the one the woman had called Andrew. He gave Cormac a look of humorous self-confidence.

Cormac meant to thank him but instead in his frustration burst out with, "His wife only just died, but no one has talked about it all night."

"I will talk about anything you wish." He put an arm around Cormac's shoulder with a quiet, casual authority. Walking the minstrel into a dark corner, he continued, "But she is boring to talk about. She always was." The lute was gently taken away and put on a small table.

"It seems a terrible way to die."

"Aye, that is so. But she left her husband's protection, so why would anyone be surprised that ill came of it?" He kissed Cormac lightly on the mouth, and Cormac knew that the kiss was the price of talking.

"You think she died because she left him?" he asked.

"At home where she belonged, she would not have wandered out into the snow, and who kens who invited or tempted her there. Does it matter?" With a knight's strength, he swung Cormac around, pressed him against the wall, took his head between his hands, and kissed him more deeply.

The increasing rasp of Cormac's breath seemed to blend with the vague festivities in the darkness around them. Somewhere near were a slap of flesh on flesh and a man moaning. Andrew was surprisingly good as he stroked Cormac's neck and began to unfasten his doublet. Cormac caught his hands and whispered softly in his ear, "Mayhap Dunbar tried to take her home and she ran out into the snow."

"No, we were still in Stirling that night with the king's party."

He nipped at Cormac's neck, but Cormac slithered and squirmed until he was loose from Andrew's hold and grabbed his lute. The man would be annoyed to have been led on, but such was life.

Andrew grasped his arm and said, "Where are you going?"

"'Tis time for me to leave."

"But..."

Cormac patted Andrew's cheek. "You're braw, mo caraidh." He stepped toward the door. "But I must be away."

"But... but..." Andrew yelped behind him. "You must nae say anything... If anyone kent..."

Cormac turned and put a finger to his lips. "Wheesht. No one shall. Forbye, what happens in the dark disnae count in the daylight." He hurried out and let the door close softly behind him.

In spite of being wrapped in his heaviest cloak and his plaid and pacing up and down the dark vennel, Law's hands and feet were numb with cold. The knife-sharp wind had slashed his face raw. Twice he'd ducked out of sight from being spotted by the watch. It had been too long. Something must have happened, he was sure, so he warily sneaked toward Dunbar's house. When he reached the gate, it was swung open. He made out a shape. "Cormac?" he whispered.

"Law? Are you daft?" The minstrel hurried to him and put a hand on his arm. "A Dhia, you're frozen."

Law put his arm around Cormac's shoulder to hurry him along toward home, and his warmth felt like heaven. "Are you all right?"

"I am fine." He made a sound that could have been a snort or a laugh. "What a sad feast. But I think I learnt what you need."

Law shared his long plaid with Cormac, whose cloak was not as thick as it could be. "Tell me, but let us hurry, before we're both frozen."

"There was a woman who seemed very familiar with Dunbar. She's his regular leman, I suspect, but I had nae chance to talk to her. She was climbing all over him the whole time. A man there, Andrew they called him, said they were all with the king's party in Stirling the night that Jannet died."

"You think he was telling the truth?"

Cormac chuckled. "He had other things on his mind than lying. Aye, it was the truth." He chuckled again, but it sounded a bit sad. "I dinnae think he's a bad man. Pathetic and foolish. They are trying so hard to be evil but are just vain men who have to pay for their pleasure."

Law looked at Cormac but could not make out his face. "We should hurry."

"Only a little farther." They turned the corner and light from the windows of the inn lit up the vennel like a beacon. "Did you learn anything from the song maister?"

"He wasn't what I expected. Hearty and burly, an odd man for the post. But aye. He telt me something that will help.

His house is near where she died, and he thinks that is why she was yon."

Cormac pushed off the half of Law's plaid he had shared, stepped away, and opened the door of the inn. "Then we are both good spies. Let us celebrate with a drink where it is warm."

5

Law squatted beside Saint John's Street in the shadow of the church's high bell tower, closely examining the ground. No trace of blood. You would never have known a body had lain there only a few minutes before.

Sergeant Meldrum gazed at Law with unhappy exasperation. "Devil take you, Sir Law, I cannae take your feeling on the matter to the lord sheriff."

"I only said it is too odd a happenstance."

"I see nothing odd about it. Maister Kennedy left the song school after dark, although his desk was piled with papers. Brother Hugh said that probably meant that Maister Kennedy intended to return. He was particular about leaving papers in order, the friar said. With a high fire burning in his office, he probably wanted a bit of fresh air. So he was walking down the street in the dark and slipped on the ice. His head slammed into a cobblestone, and he froze to death before he came to." Meldrum pointed to the frozen ground. "I saw you slip a bit as you walked up. He was an older man, more likely to fall."

"And I'm a lame one, but I did not. Moreover, I saw the letter in which Jannet told her father about being close to Kennedy. He admitted to me that he gave her a key to his little house in the north suburb. I am sorry, Meldrum. I still say two people who kent each other well freezing to death in less than a week is too odd a coincidence." Law rubbed his hands together to warm them. "You really think he would go out walking in the wind we had last night?"

"Clearing his head, no doubt, as I said. Or walking as he thought about his problems. It was too late to call upon a student's family, and Vespers had rung so most priests and brothers were at their prayers."

"He was tied to Jannet Neyn Patrik Ross's death."

"How? That he gave her a key to his house? Are you saying he killed her? That makes no sense since he is dead as well. Do you have even a mite of information to show that he had anything to do with it?" When Law shook his head no, Meldrum went on. "The lord sheriff telt you to look into it so I have not made up my mind, but you have to come to us with more than guesses. What evidence do you have? Any?"

"No."

"I need to go to the Tolhouse and wait for Sir William. This cannae be put aside as Jannet Neyn Patrik Ross's death was. The assize will declare it an accident this very day."

Law grimaced. "I shall go with you. I need to find out whether Jannet still had that key that Kennedy said he gave her before she died."

The heavy door of the Tolhouse banged closed behind them. "When do you think the lord sheriff will be here?"

Meldrum was unwinding his long plaid from his shoulders

and shaking it out. "I dinnae ken. Soon, since it's the song maister."

The body already lay draped with white linen on a trestle in the middle of the vast chamber. A priest, a thin, gawky man at the head, murmured a prayer. When Law reached the table and pulled back the sheet to expose Kennedy's face, the priest gasped. "What are you doing? Leave him be!"

Kennedy's head lay strangely askew from his body. With two fingers, Law tilted his head even farther to expose the man's cheek more fully. "Look." He laid his hand on a mottled bruise, not dark, but distinct. "That is a handprint. You can even make out the fingers. It was never made by a cobble."

Meldrum made a dismissive spluttering sound. "It would nae have killed him either."

Law walked, beaming, around the table. He spread his arms wide. "My old friend. You are right. Certes, it would not." He reached Meldrum and pulled him into a vigorous hug, slapping his back. Law reached up and patted the startled Meldrum's cheek. He grabbed it and shoved Meldrum's head back. He twisted it a bit. Meldrum yelped and tried to squirm but was held fast in Law's grip.

A guard from the door ran toward them, shouting to stop.

Law still smiled, but his teeth were bared. "You'd be dead or at least unconscious and dying if I wanted." He threw his hands up and stepped back, still smiling. "Are you so sure he froze to death, Sergeant?"

A banging made Law turn his head. Sir William Ruthven of Balkernoch, Lord Sheriff of Perth, slammed his hand down on a table on the dais. He shouted, "What is this to-do?"

Meldrum was red-faced with a furious glower. "I thought you were a knight. Why would you ken such a trick?"

"In France, the Douglas had us mostly fight afoot as we were the day he died in battle. I learnt every trick that I could to stay alive."

"What trick? And what has that to do with the song maister being dead?" the lord sheriff demanded.

Law wiped the false smile from his face and walked toward him. "What it has to do with the song maister is that his neck was broken, probably just about how I showed your sergeant. You can have the body looked at by the canon from Saint Leonard's, or the Blackfriars must have an infirmarer. But it's clear that was not a fall that left him unconscious. No fall on cobblestones ever snapped someone's neck and left a handprint on his face."

"Merciful Saints," the sheriff muttered.

Meldrum frowned thoughtfully. "So he would have already been dead."

"Possibly, but it may have taken him a while to die. You'd be surprised how hard it is to kill someone instantly." Law pulled the sheet up to cover the dead man's face. "He may have been unconscious as he died. Probably."

"This disnae prove anything about the woman's death," the lord sheriff said.

"He said he agreed to help her because of her consanguineous marriage. He telt me he gave her a key to a house he owned near where she died and for some papers there for the dissolution of her marriage. That was the day before her death. If you believe his story, which I did not."

Meldrum held up his hand in protest. "Hold. Are you accusing him of her death?"

"No, not that. He was at the song school until well after the storm hit, so I don't think it was even possible for him to reach where she died. But he was lying about other matters, what was between them for one and about why she went to the house."

The lord sheriff nodded slowly. "She was his leman."

The priest, who'd been looking back and forth between

them in silence, yelped in protest, but a glare from the lord sheriff silenced him once more.

"From what the canoness said, that much was obvious. Nor does the story about sending to Rome make sense. You ken the gold that would take. Where would he find it? Forbye, if there had been papers he could have given them to her or sent them by messenger if he was worried about scandal. No, there was something else there that she went for, though if she reached the house or not, I dinnae ken." He looked at Meldrum. "Was there a key with her when she was found?"

"I must admit I dinnae remember. Nothing seemed unusual to catch my attention, no coin or the like, except for a gimmel ring on her ring finger." Meldrum motioned to the guard. "Bring her belongings here from the kist in my office."

The priest was twisting his fingers together in distress. "I need to go to the bishop. He must be hearing of this immediately." At the lord sheriff's nod, he scurried out the door.

"This is a disaster," the lord sheriff said, grimly. "The king will be drawn into it. The song maister is a position of importance. And you ken the king is already quarreling with the pope."

"I must find this house of Kennedy's and see if anything in it throws light on the mess. He was not meeting Jannet there, so why would he send her? That puzzles me mightily."

"You did not ask him?"

"Of course not. I did not let on that I thought he was lying, the better to convince him to keep talking. I planned to go back after I'd snooped more, hopefully with something to use to trip him up."

"Her death still may have been an accident, although..." The lord sheriff rubbed the back of his neck thoughtfully. "With this I think we can agree she did not harm herself. It may have had nothing to do with Kennedy, except that he sent her to her death."

"Possibly, but how likely is it—?" Law broke off when the guard appeared in the doorway with a bundle of cloth in his arms.

Sir William pointed to a round table on the dais, and the guard dumped the load of cloth onto it. The lord sheriff nodded permission, so Law began to poke through them. There was a heavy woolen cloak and a woolen checked gown, the sort often worn by Highland women, wrapped around a pair of sturdy shoes. Perhaps she'd chosen the simple gown because of the approaching storm that day. She had been dressed as one who knew Highland weather would when a storm was in the offing.

When he lifted the gown, a small leather scrip, the sort one used to carry a few coins or a bit of bread, fell from within its folds. Law picked it up and loosened the ties. As Meldrum had said, there were no coins—though there might have been, Law thought, when the body was found. No way to tell now. But he dumped a key into his palm. He held it up for the others to see.

"I had no reason to pay heed to that," Meldrum said in a defensive tone.

"And wouldn't have kent what door it would fit if you'd paid heed to it. We need to ken if she ever reached the house. Or if whatever she was seeking is still yon. Or what she took there. It might answer some of our questions."

The lord sheriff's face was drawn into a fierce scowl. "I want those answered before the king's chancellor comes down upon me like an avalanche. So see to it."

Law tilted his head and quirked his mouth into a smile. "I dinnae think that Ross will pay for my investigating Kennedy's murder, Sir William." He bounced the key casually in his hand.

"Wheesht, man. I expect the bishop will do that." At Law's raised eyebrow, he continued, "If he disnae, then I shall. Now be off with you. Hie to that house now and come back with some answers."

"I want to see as well," said Meldrum. The two stepped together through the door and into an icy drizzle. Law muttered a curse.

Bundled in their differing plaids over their heavy cloaks, they hurried to the Northgate Port. Once through the gate, Law pointed to a small house with a fenced plot before the door. "That has to be it." All the other houses in sight had lights inside and wisps of smoke from hearth fires against the day's bitter cold.

The garden was still snow covered, but there was a trampled path through it past the bare limbs of a rose tree on one side and a wooden shelter stacked with kindling on the other. Inside the gate, Law squatted to examine the trampled ground. Someone had been through the garden more than once since the storm. They'd trampled the snow down, but it had refrozen to a hard layer since they passed.

"Whoever was here, it was after Jannet died and long enough for it to freeze hard."

Meldrum stamped the slush loose from his feet and motioned toward the door. "Let us see whether the key fits. Why would he bother with a lock on such a small house? What was he hiding, I wonder."

Law straightened and walked carefully over the icy path to the door. The key went in easily enough, but it was a bit of a struggle to make the frozen lock turn. Then it clicked. Law pushed the door open and stepped over the threshold. Inside it was dim, and he went to the window and threw open the shutters. The watery daylight did little to help.

Law looked about. The room was well furnished. There was a settle with velvet cushions, a good-sized table with nothing on it except a lamp, four stools, and a cold brazier in the corner. The walls were paneled with good pine. On the other side of the room was an inner door that swung open at Law's touch.

Within was shadowy, and Law peered about into the murk. At the foot of a box bed with red damask hangings was a carved wooden kist, and beside an empty hearth stood a chair.

"If anyone has been inside, they left no sign," said Meldrum.

"Aye. If the house was searched, it was neatly done. Or what they searched for was easily found. We'll need to search ourselves to see whether anything is hidden."

Meldrum went to the only window and opened the shutters. "I'll light that lamp in the other room, so we can see what we are about."

When the sergeant returned with the lamp, Law decided to begin in the easiest place and threw open the lid to the kist. On top was a doublet of heavy blue samite, not folded but carelessly tossed in; below that, a good furred man's houppelande with long, scalloped-edged sleeves and a furred cloak were balled up. Law raised an eyebrow at the rich attire and draped them over the lid of the kist. They were fine quality and little worn, if they had been worn at all. By the time he reached the large scrip at the bottom of the kist, he had pulled out eight garments, roughly handled for such good quality.

"Och! That is promising," said Meldrum.

Law shook his head and upended the empty purse. With little hope of success, he used the lamp to look under the bed and behind it and even up the chimney flue. He found nothing but dust.

Meldrum dusted his hands after crawling on the floor. "What do you think?"

"I think a number of things." He replaced the garments in the kist more neatly than he had found them. "But nothing I am ready to say aloud."

"We could bring one of my men to pull up the boards of the floor," the sergeant said doubtfully.

"We'd not find anything. Why ever he sent Jannet, he did nae expect her to pull up boards. No, I think it was in that scrip."

"Then what happened to it? She did nae have anything of note when her body was brought to the Tolhouse. You think the lad who found her body took it?"

Law studied Meldrum thoughtfully.

The man's face flushed a fiery red. "Dinnae you look at me so. I am no thief."

"No." Law rubbed his chin. "I have heard things about you, but not that you are a thief. And the lad who found her was too frightened to steal from a dead body. That seems certain. So the person who trampled the snow in the garden must be the one who has whatever Kennedy sent Jannet for. Or sent her with. But..."

"But...?"

Law nodded to himself. "But a number of things are far less than clear. Let us be off before it's full dark. There are people I must speak to."

6

Inside Reidheid's Hostelry, the air smelt pleasantly of ale and roasting meat. The innkeeper hurried up with a bow and led them to a table in a corner. From his broad shoulders, the brown robe swung around Brother Hugh's strong stride.

"Hoi, Brother Hugh, what are you doing away from the song school?" said someone as they passed. "Brother Hugh, good to see you," someone else called out. The friar bobbed a friendly nod.

After they sat down, Hugh gave Law a modest smile. "I dinnae have a chance to go out to an inn often, Sir Law. This is an indulgence for me. Especially with the confusion at school for now."

The innkeeper brought a pitcher of ale with two cups and said, "Brother Hugh, I heard the boys were sent home from school. That's a shame. When do you think it will open again?"

"It is all gone agley with the maister's death. It is up to the bishop to decide. I'd nae want to say." He motioned to Law. "And this is Sir Law, acting as the lord sheriff's man."

"Och, Sir Law and I have met afore." He gave Law a doubtful look before he glanced back to the friar. "The mutton stew is good the day."

"Do you have a bean potage? Feasting with the poor maister lying dead..." He shook his head. "Nae, it would not be fitting."

"We always have potage on the back of the fire. Some good bread with it and it will do you nicely."

"Two then," Law said, not bothering to clarify that he was hardly in the service of the lord sheriff and regretting a hearty mutton stew. "I'm fine with a potage."

When the innkeeper walked away, Brother Hugh looked seriously at Law with candor in his wide blue eyes. "You were very insistent about bringing me out with you, Sir Law."

Law leaned toward him. "The lord sheriff has tasked me with looking into Maister Kennedy's murder."

"Into what?" His face tightened with shock. "You must be jesting. No one would murder the maister of the song school. Why would they? And if they did, why, it would be on everyone's tongue. He fell and was helpless against the freezing cold. That's all. A very sad thing, but it could nae have been murder."

"Why could it not be?"

"Why..." For a moment, the friar sat open-mouthed. "I suppose it could be, but I heard there were no wounds on him, so how could it? And I still say there would be no reason to kill him, a priest. You must be jesting."

"I swear to you that I am not. This is a grave matter. I believe he had information about Jannet Neyn Patrik Ross that would have explained much about her death. You ken that I talked to him in the afternoon. But I was to return today to talk to him more."

To Law's annoyance, the innkeeper chose that moment to set a big bowl of steaming bean potage down in front of each of them. The interruption made it hard to judge Brother Hugh's reaction. The friar gave the thick soup a stir with his spoon and took a mouthful. "What could Maister Kennedy have telt you about that since he was at the school the night that she died?"

"That is not what I need to talk to you about. When I went by the school, one of the students told me they sought you after vespers and could nae find you."

The spoon paused on its way to the friar's handsome mouth. He looked annoyed. "You were asking about me?"

"I was asking whether they saw anything unusual. The lad mentioned it to me. Where were you going so late?"

"I dinnae ken that it is any of your business, but I'll think on it." He steadily scooped up the bean potage, keeping his eyes on the bowl all the while. When the bowl was empty, he pushed it away and laid his arms on the table. "I had planned to go to the lord sheriff with this, but since he is having you look into it, I suppose it is as well to tell you. Last night after Vespers, I went back to finish some work. Sir Archibald Dunbar came looking for the song maister. You can check. Someone had to have let him in, for the doors were already locked. He had been drinking, a great deal I suspect. He was beside himself, blathering on that Jannet's death was Maister Kennedy's doing. He said people were blaming him for what he had nae done. I told him there was nothing I could do about it, but he wanted me to tell him where Maister Kennedy was."

Brother Hugh contemplated his empty bowl for a moment. "I told him that Maister Kennedy had gone out. Dunbar was almost violent. He grabbed me by the arms and said he would make me tell him where Kennedy was. I pushed him away and told him to get hold of himself. How dare he threaten a friar? He seemed to come to himself then. So he left. I dinnae ken if he went seeking the song maister or no. I prayed in the chapel to calm myself and then went to my cell to sleep. And this morning I learned that Maister Kennedy had fallen and died."

The friar looked at Law with a touch of indignation in the tight lines of his mouth. Law could see the white skin of his tonsure surrounded by the curling locks of his blond hair. The sleeves of his robe pushed back slightly exposed cords of muscles in his arms and a sprinkling of fine hairs. Law's own image was reflected back at him in the earnest blue eyes.

"Thank you for explaining that to me."

Brother Hugh shrugged. "I had to tell you what happened."

Law shook his head. "All right, Brother Hugh. That is all I had to ask you."

"It is daft to think that the woman was murdered. Do you think Maister Kennedy was murdered too?" He narrowed his eyes and leaned forward to stare into Law's face. "Are you thinking that I did it?"

"The idea had occurred to me."

"You have an evil mind, Sir Law. I should be angry, but instead I shall pray for you. I live a godly life by the commandments and the rule of Saint Benedict. Have you told this crazy idea to anyone else?"

"There are several people I must consider might have done it. I've drawn no attention to considering you."

"Then no harm done, I suppose, as long as scandal is nae attached to the Church."

"Do you think the Church is damaged by Kennedy's relationship with Jannet?"

The friar's lips thinned and his eyes widened until Law could see the whites of his eyes around the iris. "She was a whore. It was Satan's work that a priest like Maister Kennedy could nae see that. But it is her soul that was blackened with sin. It had nothing to do with the Church or with me. I am sorry that anyone must suffer the fires of Hell, but she deserves it for a lustful life."

The sound of a chuckle made Law look up. A thin, wiry man stood a few feet from their table.

Now the man's dark hair was combed out of his eyes, no longer stringy as it once had been. The man's clothes were no longer ragged. Instead they were a simple, sturdy, hodden-gray; he might have passed for a journeyman worker. But the sharp eyes had not changed at all. Law shoved his stool back and jumped to his feet. He glared at Dave Taylor, whom he'd once known as a lowly rat catcher.

"You," Law growled, clenching his fists.

And then Brother Hugh was walking briskly away. Law cursed.

"Sorry I lost you your preaching friar." Dave Taylor smirked.

"That's not all you lost me, you sleekit thief." Law narrowed his eyes at the thief, who sidled to the other side of the table well out of reach. "Where is that damned cross that you stole?"

The former rat catcher put up his empty hands. "You dinnae think I still have it?" He pondered Law for a moment. "No, you will not take the cost out of my hide. Instead, you should talk to my employer. And he wants to talk to you."

"Dinnae be so sure I won't take it out of your filthy hide whoever your employer might be."

Dave considered Law, and an acid smile appeared. "You had best hear what he has to say first."

"Who?"

Dave looked quickly around. He shook his head. "I'll nae say the name here. Just come with me."

Law snorted. "You expect me to go with you somewhere? What for? A knife in the back?"

"Now why would I be doing that?" He laughed softly. "There would be no coin in it for me, you ken."

"Why should I trust you?"

"You're really afeart of me? I dinnae think so."

Law dropped his hand to the dirk in his belt. "No, that I am not. Very well. You've made me curious. I shall talk to this employer of yours, but there is a debt between us, and I mean to collect."

Dave Taylor, still a rat catcher in Law's mind, set off into the street. Law fell in beside him. After several days of bad weather, there were carts moving through the street and rowdy cries echoing through the market. Laborers hurried to catch up on work that had gone undone. A burly wife carrying the body of a large goose under her arm jostled him aside, grumbling on his lack of good sense as she passed.

They turned into the courtyard of a sprawling stone house and stopped at the foot of a stair tower. "You ken whose house this is, I suppose."

Law grunted and stepped toward the door. When he turned to tell the rat catcher that he was not done with him, he was gone. Through gritted teeth, Law growled, "Sleekit weasel. One day he'll pay."

He stood before the house of Robert de Cardeny, whose steward had employed him so recently. When the bishop was in Perth, as he often was, this was where he stayed. Law looked thoughtfully over his shoulder, watching Dave saunter away. It was not Bishop de Cardeny he had supposed the wily spy worked for, but he shrugged, climbing the curved stairs with their ornate railings. The steward, still in his old-fashioned tunic, waited at the top to open the door. He led Law through a short enfilade of cold rooms.

He opened the door to the last chamber.

Law's mouth dropped open when he found himself face to face with Bishop Cameron, chancellor to King James. He snapped it closed. Cameron, newly made Bishop of Glasgow by the king over the protests of the pope and no more than thirty years in age, his face chapped from the cold, was garbed for riding in mud-splashed purple velvet and high boots. From the look of him, Law must have been summoned almost as soon as the chancellor's party dismounted in the courtyard.

Now, Law thought, Dave Taylor's appearance in Perth made considerably more sense. And confirmed who he had always thought ended up with the damned cross he had sought those months before.

"I have some questions for you, Sir Law." Law knelt to kiss the bishop's ring. "You seem to have recovered well from your injuries in France." Law murmured an agreement. "I believe the sheriff has tasked you with looking into the sad death of the maister of the burgh's song school."

"Sad may not be the best word for what happened," Law parried.

"How so?"

"There were signs of violence on his body," Law said cautiously. "The marks were clearly made by a human hand, not a fall."

"That is most regrettable." John Cameron pulled a sour face. He pointed impatiently to a nearby stool. Law rose from his knees, wincing at a twinge in his scarred left leg. "Especially since funds from rent of lands the song school owns are missing from the school's coffer."

"And there is the matter of the woman."

Law started, for he hadn't noticed Robert de Cardeny, Bishop of Dunkeld and Perth, standing at the window, looking out at the gloomy skies beyond. His long, solemn face was creased with worry.

Cameron spread his dark gaze across the far end of the dimly lit room as he pondered his words. A stand of candles and a blazing brazier cut the dark and the chill, but only a little. Law shivered as Cameron picked up a goblet from the table beside him. He took a long drink of the wine, the rich scent cutting through the smell of wet wool and sweat from a long, fast ride.

"The woman..." Cameron finished his wine and sat down the goblet, "she was a Ross?"

"Aye," Law said. "A distant relation to the Lord of the Isles."

"She had left Archibald Dunbar and become friends with Kennedy," Cameron said disapprovingly. "What was the husband thinking to allow such a thing? Or the Earl of Dunbar not to keep his family's affairs in better order?"

Law shrugged.

"It is urgent we discover what happened to Kennedy and where the funds are. The scandal..." Bishop Cardeny shook his gray head. "In all my years as bishop, I have never had such a scandal."

"It will not be a scandal, Robert. I assured His Grace of that. We shall give the pope no weapon to use against us."

Law kept his tongue between his teeth. He had heard there was a serious dispute between King James and the pope. The king had appointed Cameron as bishop of Glasgow rather than accepting the pope's choice, and the disagreement between the king and the Pope was growing heated. Moreover, the king had proposed an Act of Parliament forbidding money from leaving Scotland for the church coffers in Rome. A man with good sense would stay well out of royal politics, and he considered his sense most excellent. He cleared his throat and asked, "Where were the missing coins kept?"

Bishop Cardeny gave Law a startled glance as though for a moment he had been forgotten. "In a coffer in Kennedy's privy chamber."

"If we could start at the beginning, sir," Law said. "How was it found to be missing? When?"

Bishop Cardeny paused as though setting his thoughts in order, glancing around his comfortably furnished chamber, the table covered with a silk carpet, and the silver gleam of the candle stand. At last he said, "When I received word that Kennedy was dead, I at once sent my secretary to the school to act in Kennedy's stead until I made a new appointment. I commanded him, of course, to survey the contents of the office. When he went to check the kist, it was unlocked and empty."

"Could it be elsewhere in the school?"

The bishop shook his head. "The office and his chamber and then the entire school were searched. The rents had been collected on Michaelmas past as usual. They were a substantial sum. Brother Hugh confirmed that they were received. The records will be checked, but I have no doubt he spoke truly. In the few months since, little of that would have been used."

"Enough coin that they would be difficult to conceal?"

The bishop tilted his head and thought about it. "Most like it would have fit in a good-sized scrip. If could have been concealed under a cloak or—" He frowned and shook his head. "But anyone going into Kennedy's chamber would have been seen and questioned."

Law wondered whether that were true. "I'll need to see it for myself, sir." He sighed. It was never a happy business giving powerful men bad news. "But I must tell you that Jannet was outside the Northgate Port because Kennedy sent her there himself. He admitted that to me. He sent her to retrieve something; he said papers to sue for dissolution of her marriage."

"But?" Cameron made an impatient gesture for Law to continue.

"But she had no papers with her when she died, nor were such papers in his house."

Cameron jerked his head up. "His house? Was he not a Benedictine?"

"He was a priest secular," Cardeny replied.

The two bishops exchanged grim looks.

"So he had a house?" Cameron said. "I take it you went yon."

Law nodded. "I searched it. As I said, there were no such papers in it. There was a kist containing braw clothing, a man's, velvet and fur. It all looked new, and none was clerical garb, and there was an empty scrip large enough to be what you describe."

Cameron slammed his fist on the table, making the candle stand shake. He watched as though daring it to tip over. When it had steadied, he turned to Cardeny. "I have a man who can poke about amongst the poor of the burgh to see whether anyone has coin who should not. That coin must have gone somewhere. Mayhap Kennedy had it with him and was killed for it."

Law leaned forward, elbows on his knees. "Unlikely that he would have carried so much on his person. And they would have had to ken he carried it. He had kept whatever his plans were secret from everyone...except mayhap Jannet. I am afeart the explanation may not be anything so simple." He sighed. "And may be a scandal..."

"I am afeart you have the right of it," Cameron said, "but I'll not leave any stone unturned, so my man will check."

Law grimaced. "Dave Taylor, you mean."

In a cool tone Bishop Cameron said, "I ken no one of that name."

"Ah." Law stood. "If I may, I'll go examine this kist and Kennedy's rooms. As you say, sir, we would be wise to leave no stone unturned."

Cameron gave Law a dark stare. "You are to report to me and no one else. This is a privy matter that matters greatly to His Grace the King. So keep your tongue still and come straight here when you learn anything."

Law shared a deep bow between the two men. Bishop Cameron delivered a blessing with the hand not holding the wine goblet, and waved a dismissal.

In the doorway, he put a hand on the frame and paused. He had mentioned his conversation with Patrik Ross to no one. The timing might well have been right for Ross to have found Kennedy and killed him. But surely Kennedy was killed by the same person who killed Jannet. And Ross would not have killed his own daughter. Would he? Or perhaps there were two killers. Had Law been too fast to believe that Kennedy could not have gone out the night when Jannet was killed?

"Well?" Cameron demanded.

Law looked over his shoulder at the bishop. He opened his mouth but then closed it and shook his head. "Nothing, sir. I shall return when I learn anything."

❧ 7 ❧

Beams of light from the windows of the Blackfriars Abbey broke the murk of the darkening day. The same grizzled friar as before—the porter, Law supposed—opened the gate when Law rang the bell for entrance. He frowned at Law and shook his head. "Patrik Ross did nae return last eve, if it is he you are seeking."

"It is, but if he is nae here then I must examine the guest-house where he bides."

"What?" The friar reared back as though even the mention of such a thing was an attack.

Law held up a hand and smiled. "You cannae allow it; I understand. If you will find the prior or take me to him, this is a matter that he should deal with."

The porter squinted at him suspiciously. "Why would the prior want to speak with you?"

Law sighed. "This is the bishop's business, so I have no doubt he will want to."

"Come with me then." He grudgingly led Law across the wintery lawn past the Chapter House with its arched, carved windows to the refectory where the scent of fish cooking for the next meal filled the air. The prior, a short, compact man whom Law had first met those months ago when Duncan was murdered, was deep in conversation with another friar holding a thick sheath of papers. As he approached, Law caught the tail end of a conversation about the number of barrels of salt fish in the cellar.

At first glance the prior was simply clad in his white robe and black cloak as any other, but the cross that hung from his leather girdle was jeweled, and his robe was fine wool. He raised a graying eyebrow at Law.

Law bowed respectfully, but he paused, rubbing his ear. This was a delicate matter. "Mayhap we could speak alone?"

The prior motioned to an alcove at the far side of the long, simple chamber filled as it was with trestle tables and benches where the sizeable community would dine. Law let the prior lead him there. "You ken that Ross's daughter died under strange circumstances."

"Aye. A sad matter, but it has nothing to do with us." He gave a wry twitch of his mouth. "Although that has not meant that some of the lay brothers have nae gossiped about it."

Law lowered his voice. "You may not have heard that Maister Kennedy of the song school has died as well. Been killed. Bishop Cardeny has tasked me with looking into the matter for him. The death of Ross's daughter and Kennedy's murder seem to be linked. And I am concerned if Ross did nae return last eve. I absolutely must examine the guesthouse where he is lodged."

"You spoke with Ross after his daughter died. The porter reported as much to me."

"Aye. I have in the past..." Law pondered how to put it. "I have helped work out strange matters, and her death seemed so. He asked for my aid. But this goes beyond that. If something has happened to Ross, I dinnae ken. Or if he has any connection with Kennedy's death, but if there is anything to be found in his lodging, I must find out."

The prior widened his eyes. "If he has any connection with the death? You think it was his doing?"

"I'll nae accuse a man without proof, but it is possible. I spoke to him yesterday, and he was beside himself. Furious, in fact. So I need to find evidence one way or the other. I must start here."

The prior stroked the cross that hung at his waist for a moment. "If Bishop Cardeny has approved your scrutiny into the matter, I'll nae deny you."

A moment later the porter was leading Law once more through the narrow covered passage between the large chapter house and the chapel and through the courtyard along a path now cleared of snow. He hammered at the door of the guesthouse before pushing it open. Law thanked him and firmly closed the door.

The gloomy light from the window was not enough for a proper search, so Law lit a half-burnt candle on the table. In this room, there was little to search. He pulled cushions off the settle, but the shallow box that formed the seat was empty. The door opened at Law's touch. Holding the candle high to light the shadowy room, Law took a good look about. It was a simple chamber with a box bed that did not even have hangings, a smallish kist against a wall, a bare hearth, and a stool next to a table that held only another candle. Law lit it from the one that he held.

The two cast a wavering light, so he went quickly to work. The hearth was cold. It had not been used for at least the night before, so it was likely that, as the porter had said, Ross had not been here the night before and had probably not returned after speaking to Law at Wulle's inn. He peered behind the bed, knelt to look under it, and craned to look on the top. He moved the stool to beside the kist, put one of the candles on it, and opened the lid. He quickly turned over a plaid carelessly folded, a paper with a list of goods to be purchased while in Perth, and more garments. Obviously, Ross had intended to return.

And there was no sign of a store of coins, whether belonging to the song school or anyone else.

Law quickly returned everything to where he had found it. Where was Patrik Ross then? What had he been doing since he stormed out of the inn last evening?

Sun breaking through storm clouds in the west gave the afternoon a dim, watery light. Law splashed through ice-rimed puddles toward Wulle's inn, trying to unravel the knots in all of the stories he had been told. Gusts of cold wind rattled the shutters of houses as he passed.

What Kennedy sent Jannet to retrieve or possibly to store had to have been the missing coins. Or had he planned to meet her there? A priest stealing from the church was not unheard of, but a man as well-established as Kennedy? Law shook his head. The thoughts spinning through it were giving him a headache. In no way could he imagine his present employer being pleased with the solution to the murders.

The benches of the inn were empty, and Cormac was alone sitting on a stool near the peat fire, his small lute in his lap. Notes plinked in, seeming random to Law's ear, as the minstrel tuned it. From time to time, Cormac tilted his head as he tested the strings. Cormac did not see Law until he walked around to the far end of the long room. Then he stopped and smiled up at him, pushing strands of his red hair out of his eyes.

"No custom to play for, but I've never seen you play a lute before," Law said.

"I can when I need to." He stood and carefully laid the lute on the stool. "But after being out in the cold and damp of night, it was out of tune." He walked ahead of Law to a table where he had left a pitcher and cup. He sat, poured a cup of ale, and looked up ruefully. "Did what we learnt help at all?"

"It added to the puzzle. I have a guess who the killer is, but no way to prove it. And I could be wrong. But I dinnae think so."

Cormac's eyes widened. "Who?" The minstrel was sitting, chin on his hand, head tilted, looking at Law with an intent expression.

"Think about it." Law glanced around. Mall was busy on the far side of the long room, so he continued. "Kennedy was dallying with a married woman, hardly the first priest to do so, I'll admit."

Cormac smirked.

Law chuckled. "But this was a woman who had left her husband, who was likely to at some point demand she return. One with a connection to a powerful family. So they give out the story that they're appealing to the pope for a divorce. To buy time? To satisfy her family? That I dinnae ken."

"But...?"

"But it's nonsense. And no such papers to be found, but good clothes stored at his house—not clothing of a cleric—and money gone missing from the song school." Law paused to take a drink of his ale. "No, they planned to flee together. That much is clear. I suspect taking the money there to hide was the reason he gave her the key. But why did she go out there that morning when the weather was so ill? Kennedy admitted he hadn't expected her to do so. She was lured out there. Mayhap with a false message from him. But for that to happen, it had to be someone who kent about the house. Someone who kent that they met there."

Cormac was frowning, forehead creased. He shook his head. "You're sure it was nae Kennedy who killed her and his death an accident?"

"Och, his death was murder. The bruise on his face showed that clear enough. So I had to ask, who might have kent about his little house and that she could be lured yon? Someone who must have learnt that coin was missing from the song school."

Cormac leaned forward. "You mean...? Someone from the school itself? Brother Hugh? Would Brother Hugh have kent about the coin though?"

"I believe so."

"Why kill her? Why kill Kennedy?"

"He's a bit crazed. The church is always preaching about women bringing sin into the world, but when he starts about it, the hairs raise on the back of my neck." He snorted. "But I dinnae think that is going to convince Bishop Cameron that a friar is the killer. And...I still could be wrong. All I have is that I dinnae see how it could be anyone else, hardly convincing. Nor have I found Patrik Ross."

Cormac chewed his lip as he considered Law's suppositions. "But why kill Kennedy?"

"Kennedy was no fool even if he was a bad priest. He could deduce what I have. Either he confronted Brother Hugh with the deed, or the friar realized that Kennedy had guessed. And if he is as crazed as I think, killing a sinning priest might not even give him pause."

"The money? What about that? He's a friar, so he would hardly have any chance to use it, not without being caught."

"He took the money, but that wasn't why he killed them. Mayhap he meant to return it, or mayhap he just took it because he thought they shouldn't have it. He thinks...it was a good thing to kill Jannet. And he probably had to kill Kennedy to keep from being caught. Or mayhap because he was a sinner. But he's been both bold and clever."

"So..." Cormac's eyes brightened, and Law shook his head with a touch of despair. "To convince the bishop, we need proof. What do we do now?"

"First I start a search for Patrik Ross. I need to find out where he is and why he's disappeared."

"You cannae suspect him."

Law shrugged.

"But Jannet was his daughter!"

With a grim pull of his mouth, Law said, "He wouldn't be the first man in the world to put family honor above one of his children."

"Surely not."

"I dinnae think that is what happened, but I must be certain. This is no matter where guesses are enough. If he were dead, I think his body would have turned up." Law rolled his eyes and grimaced. "With the rat catcher back, I'm nae certain of anything."

"What?"

Law had to laugh. "Did I nae tell you? He is indeed Bishop Cameron's man, though that is not something the bishop cares to have commonly kent."

Cormac's eyes narrowed with a fierce look. He had good reason for ill feeling toward the rat catcher, considering he'd attacked Cormac to obtain the infamous cross. "You cannae trust that man."

"Och, that I dinnae." Law stood and smiled at his indignant friend. "There must be a way to prove Brother Hugh is the killer, and I'll find it. But first I must find Ross."

Brother Nevan said, "Brother Hugh go out? Not through this door, not last night. No one goes through without my opening it. And no one touches the key except me. Not that there aren't other ways out of the school. Any of the school lads can tell you 'tis possible to clamber over a wall if you can climb a tree." He shook his head. "But Brother Hugh? He would never do that. He is a good friar, always at his prayers. Almost Saintly." He crossed himself. "I hope it's no sin to say such. But he would never sneak out."

"But others do climb a wall. Mayhap there is a conveniently placed tree?"

"Och, aye. I ken all about lads who go scampering off after the lassies in the town every chance that they get, chasing after anything that wears a skirt. They are lads. What can you do? But Brother Hugh is nae like that."

"This is just checking on anyone who was close to Maister Kennedy. I'm not saying Brother Hugh did anything wrong."

The friar tilted his bony head toward Law, a suspicious look in his hollow eyes. "Making a chance to blame one of us for what we never did, is what you're up to. You might as well give up, Sir Law, because neither you nor anyone else is going to find that Brother Hugh did anything sinful."

"You have the wrong idea, Brother Nevan. I'm just trying to clear things up about Maister Kennedy's death."

"Well, Brother Hugh is a saintly man. So best you best go find someone else to blame for whatever evil you are thinking happened."

After Law stepped out of the door, he turned and spoke to the shadowy figure within. "By the way, did you see Maister Kennedy that night that night?"

"Of course. I told you, no one leaves that I dinnae open the door."

"Did he say anything to you?"

There was a thoughtful pause. "He said... I admit it was an odd thing to say. He said not everyone was always as they seem."

❧

Law tugged on his earlobe, scratched his ear and sighed. He had put off looking for Ross as long as he could. What would Law have done in Ross's place? This was a waste of his time, but he had to be sure the man was still alive, so he started at Dunbar's house and stopped at every inn that had a pole out showing it was serving ale. They bustled with people preferring to stay out of the snow, noisy with laughter and men shouting for service.

The third one Law stepped into, air ripe with peat smoke and the fumes of spilled drink, he spotted Ross slumped in a corner clutching a cup. He was staring into it as though the secrets of life and death were drowned in the cup.

Law stopped the innkeeper and slipped him a coin. "How long has he been here?"

The innkeeper shook his head. "He passed out on the floor last night. Kept going on about his lass and cursing at one of the Dunbars."

Law went to slide onto the bench beside Ross. "You have better things to do than this, man."

Ross raised his gaze, eyes bloodshot and bleary, but he seemed less drunk that Law had expected. "I went to her husband's house. He laughed at me. Said it was my fault for not rearing her right. He shoved me down the steps and slammed the door in my face."

Law squeezed Ross's shoulder. "It was nae your fault. Her death was nae even his. I ken who to blame, but for now you need to see to her burying. I'll talk to the sheriff, and she can have the proper rites. But you need to be sober and decent for that."

Ross let out a gusty, ale-scented sigh and nodded. When Law rose, he squeezed Ross's shoulder again. "I'll talk to you on the morrow."

It was time to put an end to this, but he had to make a plan. Deep in thought he walked home where Cormac quietly followed him up the narrow stairs.

Law paced back and forth across his small room. The minstrel sat on Law's narrow cot, hunched over, elbows on his knees. Head tilted, he watched Law.

"He's such a...sunny, happy-looking friar. They won't believe it without proof. I don't ken what I can do next. Look for the coin, but where? Try to trap him somehow. I dinnae ken exactly. But he's dangerous. And when they look at him, no one will believe it. That is the most dangerous thing about him."

Cormac frowned. "I suppose you are right. The bishop will have to have certain proof of it. Will Brother Hugh have to be tried in an ecclesiastical court?"

Law stopped his pacing long enough to shrug. "He's only a friar, nae a cleric, a priest, so possibly not. I'm nae sure what they'll do with him. If we can prove he's the killer."

"But how do we do it?" Cormac asked.

"I have to lure him out. He's killed enough that I doubt he'll stop now. I've given away that I suspect him. If I can tempt him into attacking me, that would be proof."

A smile bloomed across Cormac's face. "I have a better idea. You said he kens that you suspect him, but I could lie to him to trap him. If he killed Kennedy because Kennedy threatened to expose him, what would he do if I told him I saw him do the killing? I could demand the money and say he has to show me where it was."

Law turned and scowled down at Cormac. If there was

ever anyone who didn't look like a fighter it was his brightly dressed, smiling friend. "I will nae let you take a risk like that, Cormac. No."

"It would nae be such a risk. Jannet and Kennedy did nae ken that Brother Hugh was going to try to kill them. I do. I'll be on my guard and..." He grinned at Law. "I do expect you to stay nearby to save me."

"I dinnae like it. It would be better if I did it."

Cormac straightened and shook his head. "He would nae believe you. There is no way you saw him that night. It has to be me."

"I'd rather..."

"You've talked to him too many times. He's never seen me. It would be more believable a sneaky Hieland minstrel would be out on a dark night spying on him. That he'll believe."

Suddenly they heard a roaring wind. Law opened the shutters to look to the east. A heavy curtain of black clouds was speeding toward them. The fringes of wind hit, speeding flurries of snow into his face. He slammed the shutter closed and latched it. Within minutes, it was dark and cold. The hard pounding of the wind against the walls and roof seemed to cut off the world.

Cormac came to stand next to Law and put a hand on his arm. "Let me try."

Cormac was right, but it didn't mean he had to like it. "If you promise to be careful and do exactly as I say."

"I promise. I'll be careful. Very careful."

Law arrived at the song school while the morning was still dark, only a sliver of light breaking above the horizon. The storm of the night before had blown through, but the ground was once again covered with a thick layer of snow. Since the bishops had approved Law's searching Kennedy's office and the school, Brother Nevan only glowered a bit when he let him in.

Law gave the friar a hard stare. "The bishops would prefer that no one hear about my movements. It's best there be as little scandal as possible, so dinnae mention that I've been here. Not to anyone. If anyone needs to hear about it, leave that to bishops."

The gaunt-eyed friar nodded, and Law could only hope it was enough for Brother Hugh not to learn of his presence. He walked, soft-footed, through the hall and Brother Hugh's little office, and into Maister Kennedy's. He swung the door back and forth to be sure it didn't creak before he pulled it so that it would appear to be closed. Once Cormac arrived, he would push it open a crack to watch.

Law was sure that Brother Hugh would follow the same pattern as he did before. He must have made an appointment with Jannet. Law suspected he must have agreed to meet Kennedy away from the school to talk or the priest wouldn't have left late at night.

The morning dragged as the sky outside slowly lightened. It felt as though an entire day had gone by although it must have only been an hour when he heard the slap of sandals on the floor, the scrape of a chair, and papers rustling. Law breathed as softly as he could. The last thing they wanted was for Brother Hugh to realize Law was here.

He heard Cormac say, "I need to talk to you a while."

He eased the door open a finger's width so he could spy out.

Brother Hugh looked up. He stilled, his back stiffening. "Why? You have no business with the school."

Cormac softly closed the door behind him. "No. But I have business with you." He gave a wry smile. "You see, minstrels are often about late in the night, as I was."

The friar gave a heavy sigh, running his hands through his hair and across his tonsure. He sounded sad when he said, "The sins... They just keep piling up. We pray and pray to rid the world of them, but then there are more. But I suppose a minstrel is always sinful, so I should nae be surprised."

Cold crept up Law's spine.

"That was why you killed Maister Kennedy?" Cormac asked softly. "To stop the sin? And Jannet?"

"I *what*?" He sounded genuinely shocked.

"I saw you sneaking about before he was killed. You were following him."

Brother Hugh stood and took a turn around the chamber, his expression brooding and angry. "You could nae have seen me."

"But I did."

Brother Hugh shook his head sadly. "This is a foolish trick. Do you think I have money that you can blackmail me? I am a friar. Even my robe belongs to the order. If you say you saw me, you are lying. Or you are crazed and imaged it."

"You were walking toward where Maister Kennedy's body was found."

He looked at Cormac, his handsome face alight with indignation and virtue, smile lines enclosing his firm mouth and a little blond stubble on his cheeks. The sleeves of his robe were pushed back to expose the corded muscles of his forearms as he clasped his hands in a prayerlike pose. He was as unlikely a murderer as Law could imagine.

Cormac stared the friar down.

"You have no right to question me so, but let me think for

a moment." Brother Hugh went back to his chair, sat, and put his elbows on his desk. "I was thinking of telling that Sir Law about this. Do you ken him?"

"I've seen him in the inn where I play."

"Mayhap you can help me with this. There may even be a reward for finding money that is missing." He licked his lips and continued, "I believe I ken who did these murders, and you can help me prove it. You did nae see me, but one person in a friar's robe looks much like another. In the dark, how could you tell? Meet me near the house that belonged to Maister Kennedy where the Town Ditch runs nearby. I am sure I ken where there is evidence. It had to be someone who kent the maister well, and that will tell us who."

Cormac squinted at Brother Hugh. "How would there be evidence there?"

"The money must be somewhere, aye? That is where it is hidden and something there will show who hid it."

"Why would there be evidence? That makes nae sense."

"I believe it is in the river not far from that house. The killer put it in a casket and sunk it there. Whoever the casket belongs to is the killer. I believe I shall recognize it. All we have to do is find it."

"Then why not say who this casket belongs to?"

The friar crossed himself. "That would be a sin, to accuse someone without proof. Once we have it, I shall ken. Then you can take it to the lord sheriff and claim a reward." His voice hardened. "Unless you try to blame me for it again."

Cormac smiled. "You think he'd believe a minstrel over a friar?"

Brother Hugh nodded slowly as though thinking it over. "Meet me out there at the Town Ditch near Maister Kennedy's house. I have to bide here a while, or there will be questions. It will have to be late, near nightfall, and I'll show you where it is. They deserved what happened to them, sinners that they were." His voice got a hard, singsong quality. "The evil shall perish. Thus it must be." Then his voice became normal again. "But I shall nae let you blame me for the killing."

Cormac stared at Brother Hugh, sitting stiffly at his desk, fists gripped atop the papers. "They did nae do anything to you," he said softly.

"They were sinners, and God's wrath was visited upon them. But what happens now is up to God as well."

His face stiff with an unreadable emotion, Cormac turned and left, softly closing the door behind him. Law softly closed the crack had peered through. When Brother Hugh led him to the hidden coin, he would be able to convince Bishop Cameron and the sheriff to... He shook his head. He wasn't sure what they would do with the crazed friar. Whether they hanged him or just locked him away in some remote monastery, it wasn't his problem.

Unless he was wrong. Perhaps he hadn't done the killing. Jannet might have hidden the money and become lost in the storm. Kennedy might have slipped and fallen. The hand-shaped bruise on his face could have been a coincidence, nothing to do with his death.

Law didn't believe that, but he had to find out.

As soon as Cormac walked out of the song school, he decided to ignore Law's instructions. Law wanted him to go back to the inn and sit on his hands while he followed Brother Hugh out to the house. Law was so convinced he could not take care of himself. He was to sit and wait and wonder, and not set foot out of the sight of Wulle and a room full of customers.

With an indignant sniff, Cormac hurried through the

slushy, snow-covered street to Wulle's inn. Midwinter, nightfall came early to Perth, so he did not have long to prepare. A bowl of Mall's thick bean pottage warmed him up. He wrapped his plaid over his cloak. He'd need both as darkness fell to keep from freezing like the poor murdered Jannet. When Wulle pointed out Cormac would receive no coin if he wasn't playing, he shrugged and left.

Cormac slogged along North Street and passed through the port gate. He wrapped his plaid tightly around his shoulders to keep out the chill of the still, bright day. The sun, already sinking toward the western horizon, reflected in a blinding sheen off the snow as he tramped along the edge of the Town Ditch. A thin layer of ice covered the water, and eddies of snow played on its surface.

When he reached the house that had belonged to Kennedy, he found a spot and scouted around. An oak tree in the front was hung with icicles. The hawthorn bushes were all heavily coated with snow, like big, white bundles. He tried the door and was surprised when it swung open. No doubt, Law had not left it unlocked, but just as obviously Brother Hugh had a key. Inside the air was almost as frigid as outside. Something warm to drink would have been nice, but Cormac just pulled a stool next to the door and opened it a sliver to watch. As the temperature dropped and the afternoon darkened, his breath plumed with fog, so he wrapped his plaid around his lower face to hide it. Besides, his nose was growing numb.

There was nothing to do but wait and think. How irate would Law be when he learned Cormac had broken his promise to follow instructions? He sniffed in a soft laugh.

8

Law allowed Brother Hugh to get well ahead of him on the way out of Perth, barely within sight as he trudged between merchants tearing down stalls and laborers wearily journeying home through the fading daylight. He pulled his cloak tight so that his clothes didn't show and slumped as he walked so that he blended better with the people around him. He didn't dare let the man entirely out of his sight. Cormac was too much at risk for that even back at the inn.

Once through the port gate, he dropped back even more, since the friar would have to pass him if he turned back for town. Cormac should be safe now. He tramped through the snowy silence of the suburb. He heard a dog bark and a sound of distant laughter. He jumped when snow dropped from a bush with a splat.

When he reached Kennedy's house, he looked around. There was no sign of Brother Hugh. The door was closed. He tried the door and then cursed himself for not having brought the key. Standing beneath the oak, he listened to the silence. He slowly paced down the slope to the edge of the town ditch to look at the ice-covered water. What to do next? Could Brother Hugh have circled around to get past him and have returned to town?

The silence had an ominous quality. The hair on the back of his neck rose. It felt as though something had happened here. He squatted and examined the edge of the ditch below. Thick along the edge stood dead weeds; the ice looked thin but undisturbed, unbroken.

As he stood, a big white-fronted goose burst from the weeds with a raucous, laughing call. He heard a squelching sound in the snow behind him. Before he could turn to see what it was, pain exploded in the back of his head from a blow, rattling his brain inside his cranium. A flash of darkness enveloped his senses. No sooner than the flash had happened, he was face down in the snow. A hand pressed his face down into the wet, cold mass. Law choked, head hammering with pain.

He twisted and saw Brother Hugh looming over him, saw the bounce of blond curls and the blue eyes, narrowed and rapt. Hugh dropped on his knees in the middle of Law's back. Law grunted with the blow. The weight pushed him back down, and he cursed.

But Law was tougher prey than poor Jannet. He bucked, pushed his hands deep in the snow, and heaved against the frozen earth.

As Law reared, the friar grabbed onto his shoulders. The friar slid sideways, half-off, and Law rolled, twisting. With a grunt, Law grabbed him around the waist, struggling to get on top. Brother Hugh let go of Law and swung a fist. Law's teeth snapped when it landed on his jaw. They rolled. Law smacked the side of his head and his shoulder on rocks. He made a dazed grab for the edge of the ditch.

His arm was grabbed and yanked loose.

The smash of ice shattering under him jarred his body, but

plunging into icy water cleared Law's head. Brother Hugh wrapped his arms and legs around Law. He threw back his head, his eyes wide, teeth bared. Law floundered, trying to get his feet under him. His feet slipped in slick mud, and he was chest deep in frigid water. He struggled, trying to get leverage to free his arms and land a blow. When his feet slipped again, he went under the water. Brother Hugh's powerful hands closed on his throat and pushed him down. He thrashed to regain his feet, grabbed the strong wrists, and yanked. Still, the friar's weight pushed him down into the muck. In the wet, he couldn't get a grip to jerk the choking hands free. His lungs spasmed in a frantic need for air as he fought. In a desperate moment, he realized the mad friar did not care if he killed them both.

His chest heaved, but in a despairing act of will he locked his throat closed. He jerked on the wrists again, digging his nails into the skin to find a grip. He tore the hands away. Finally free, he twisted to get his feet under him. As he fought upward toward the air and the light, Brother Hugh grabbed him and forced him down.

It had taken too long. His breath expelled in a noisy eruption and he sucked his lungs full of icy water. At once he was in a dark dream. His lungs seemed to scream with the agony. Above was the icy sheen of the surface as darkness closed in around him.

Hard fingers dug into his throat. As he faded like a lamp burning out, he felt Brother Hugh clutch him like a lover. He had his muscular legs wrapped around Law's hips. Brother Hugh reared back, his face fierce, bucking his hips in a savage, deadly mockery of making love. With a surge of rage, Law thought of the friar leaving him here in this blue, frigid world to go after Cormac. His hand floated before his face, and with a last desperate effort, he swung it toward Brother Hugh's throat. It hit. He chopped again and then again.

Brother Hugh surged away in an eruption of waves. Law raised both feet and pushed feebly into Hugh's chest. It thrust him into a dazzling, bright world. He vomited up a gush of water. He choked and gagged, but in the glittery sunlight he saw the edge of the ditch only a steps away. He surged through the chest-high water, feet sliding and skidding in the muck; he coughed and heaved.

Brother Hugh thrashed to the surface beside Law. He steadied himself in the water, his face fixed in a rictus of fury. He lunged, hands outstretched, going for Law's throat. Law grabbed him by his robe, saw in the bright sunlight the man's strong chest where the robe had ripped away. Law pulled back his fist and swung as hard as he could...too hard, he realized with horror, when the force slid his feet out from under him. He crashed backwards, the friar on top of him. The friar's hands closed around his throat, and he went down into wintry blue darkness...

Law heaved and gagged. Water rushed out of his mouth onto the ground. Someone had him around his waist and jerked. He tried to shout for them to stop, but the jerk came again. He spewed more water and caught the fist pressed into his stomach and tried to push it away. The fist loosened, and the arms let him go.

Groaning, he rolled onto his side. He opened his eyes and looked up at Cormac's blurry face. It was pale, and hair hanging into his forehead clotted with blood. He pushed Law's hair back out of his face and said something with *mo luaidh* in it. He started to sit up, but Cormac pushed a hand against his chest to stop him. He managed to rise up on his elbows. "You're hurt," he said. "What happened?"

Maister Braidlaw, from the tannery, was suddenly beside

Cormac, shaking his head in somber disbelief. "When the dog started raising a fit and howling to raise the dead, I thought I'd better come with Gil this time. I saw the two of you flailing about in the water. Was running toward you when this lad burst out of the house yon. Just as you went under, he grabbed up a rock. He flew off the edge of the ditch like a falcon, that rock raised above his head. Down it slammed, and that was the end of the fight."

"Are you all right, Law?" Cormac asked.

Law shuddered. "He knocked me out from behind. Tried to smother me in the snow."

"That must have been what he did to Jannet," Cormac said. "There wasn't enough snow, so he left Kennedy to freeze to death."

"How did your head get bloodied?" Law asked Cormac.

"I was hiding in the house. We were supposed to meet by the Town Ditch, so I did nae think he would look yon. But he came to the house."

Law glowered at him. "I told you to wait at the inn."

"It's a good thing I ignored you." Cormac touched the bloody place on his forehead. "He was strong. We fought, and I had nae a chance. He knocked me down, I was out for a bit, must have only been a short time. When I came to, I heard the two of you out here splashing and fighting."

Law managed to get to his knees and tried to stand. Maister Braidlaw and Cormac helped him up. Another coughing fit hit him. Cormac held him up as he hacked and bent over to spit up more water. When he straightened, he saw Brother Hugh lying on his side on the ground. His hands were tied behind his back, and the tannery watchdog sat beside him, growling softly. His robe was ripped open to his waist. His blond curls were plastered to his head with water and blood.

"How did you get him tied up?" Law asked.

"He was out cold, floating in the water after the lad here clunked him on the head. Thought he was dead at first, but whilst I was dragging him out he came to. He struggled loose and tried to run, but the dog put a stop to that. Had to stop it from tearing his throat out. Gil sat on him, but he kicked Gil in the face afore I had him tied him up with the dog's rope. By that time, the lad here had you dragged onto dry land and was forcing the water out of you."

Brother Hugh growled and bared his teeth. "Aye. You should have been dead with the two of them. Both of you."

"I dinnae understand," Cormac whispered.

"They were steeped in sin. She tempted him with her harlot's ways and led him into evil. Then it was too late for him. He was so steeped in evil, he was lost, a whoremonger and a thief." He sounded sad as he continued. "At first I thought he was just weak, but when he stole from the school and planned to abscond with her, I kent there was no saving him. I was told that the only way to cleanse the school was to punish them."

Law cleared his raspy throat and asked, "Told...?"

"I have been marked to do the work of God," he said proudly. "An angel whispered to me what I must do, and I did. But I had to keep it secret."

"It is nae secret any more." He turned to Maister Braidlaw. "You'd better send Gil for the lord sheriff. This will be..." Law sighed. "It is a mess."

"Aye." Braidlaw motioned to Gil. They walked a bit away as Gil listened to his maister's instructions.

Law shut his eyes, glad Cormac was still holding him up. "I thought I was going to die this time."

"So did I," Cormac said in a low voice.

"I did nae see him at all before he hit me from behind. He knocked me out."

"I think it was the same rock that I hit him with. It already had blood on it."

"You jumped right out after him?"

"There wasn't time to think. I grabbed the rock and leapt on top of him. Slammed it down on his head."

"He attacked you first. Are you all right?"

"Aye. My head throbs a bit, but I'll live."

Law smiled a little. They both would. He looked down at the friar who was staring beyond them as though they weren't even there. Mayhap he was hearing the voice that told him to murder.

Bishop Cameron was waiting when Law arrived at the same house where they had met before. The bishop looked weary as Law kissed his ring.

He sat next to the hearth where a merry fire crackled and motioned for Law to take a seat. "What a plight. This is a scandal, and somehow I must keep it quiet." He raised his gaze to Law. "I talked to him."

"Was he...?"

"Sane? No. He was calm enough but utterly mad. He lured Jannet to the house by telling her that Kennedy wanted to meet her yon. I suppose since she kent that he was part of the song school she never suspected a thing. But when he was waiting, she ran from him into the storm. He chased the poor woman, knocked her down and smothered her in the snow." Cameron looked thoughtful. "Mayhap you would call it drowning. I'm nae sure. But he was sure he was called to do it to punish her for tempting a priest into sin. He found the money hidden in the house that night. Kennedy could hide nothing from him, though I doubt he realized that. Not until it was too late."

"Was the money there? Where he said?"

"Aye. It was part of what had tempted Kennedy into sin, so he was taking it away. Poor Kennedy got his neck broken, but he didn't leave him to freeze. You were wrong there. He was smothered whilst he lay helpless. Hugh did nae want to take a chance on Kennedy being found too soon." Cameron sighed. "I have to explain all this to the king. It will be easier to hush up if we lock him away in a safe monastery somewhere. I'll have to decide where."

Law flushed with anger. "So the murders will be covered up. What will you say about poor Jannet's death? Will she be denied even a decent burial?"

"There is nae reason for that. It was an accident. She got lost in the storm. Tragic, but such things happen. And Brother Hugh will be kept somewhere that he will be no threat to anyone."

"How can you be sure? The next time he decides someone is a sinner?"

"He will be sent to a remote monastery and watched." Cameron sighed. "He is quiet. Peaceful even. He disnae ken what is going to happen and disnae seem even to care."

"Everyone liked him, thought him almost a saint," Law said as his anger drained away. What point was there now in being angry? "I dinnae ken what is just. He is a madman."

"The King will be arriving in Perth shortly." Noises from outside the house, shouts and cheers and the tramping of horses, made the bishop turn his head. "No. He is here now, I suppose. This scandal, though hushed up, will just determine him more to bring the church in hand."

Law rose to his feet. "This ends the matter then."

"I often have business that needs attending by a man who is discreet."

"I thought you had one of those," he said in a tone sharper than was wise to use with the king's chancellor.

"Mayhap there are tasks you would be better suited for. And much of the king's business is done here in Perth."

The bishop handed Law a small leather purse, a bit lighter than Law had hoped, but he was escaping with his life—and that was more than he had expected a short time before. In the street where Cormac waited, people were lined up to watch the king ride past. He was waving and smiling beneath snapping banners, tailed by hundreds of his courtiers. Their horses pawed and snorted at the cheers of the crowd. Banners snapped above the finely clad men in a cold breeze. Law spotted both the Earl of Douglas and the Earl of Argyll in the crowd. King James still had his long-nosed Stewart good looks, but he had widened a bit at the waist since last Law had seen him. A young lass ran up to offer him an apple. He drew up his horse to take it, grinning down at her, and the people cheered their approval.

He heard Cormac snort softly. "You'd run off to follow him just like that lassie."

"I think that here is nae so bad a place to be that someone cares if I live or die, so mayhap not." He shook his head. "But Bishop Cameron may need a man to do jobs ill-suited to the rat catcher."

Cormac turned with a horrified look. "You mean to get involved with politics and lords? Tell me you will nae."

"Not if I can help it, but do you think the King's chancellor will give me a choice?"

GLOSSARY

SCOTS WORDS

Agley – askew or awry

Bairn or wean – child

Bide – stay or reside

Braw – fine or excellent

Cannae – cannot

Dinnae – did not

Disnae – does not

Fash – worry

Hielands – Highlands

Hodden-grey – Coarse homespun cloth made by mixing black and white wools

Houppelande – Outer garment, with a long, pleated body and flaring sleeves, that was worn by both men and women

Ken – know (past tense – kent)

Kist – a chest-like container or box

Lad – boy

Lassie – girl

Maister – master

Nae – not or no

Och – Oh

Outwith – outside
Plaid – a checkered blanket or wrap of woolen cloth
Sleekit – crafty, deceitful
Vennel – a minor street

Scots Gaelic Phrases

A Dhia – oh God
Clarsach – Gaelic, triangular harp
Mo luadidh – my dear
Mo caraidh – my friend

HISTORICAL NOTES

Most of medieval Perth was later destroyed, much of it by Oliver Cromwell's army, so accurately depicting the medieval layout of what was then one of Scotland's major exporting cities and de facto capital is difficult. There has been in recent years substantial excavation and research which I used and you'll find discussed in Philip Holdsworth's *Excavations in the Medieval Burgh of Perth*. Scotland's King James I, mention frequently in this novel the main character in my other novels, *A King Ensnared* and *A King Uncaged*, where I listed more of the resources I used in researching the period.

In one detail, I chose to use an anachronism. Medieval Perth was called "Saint Johnstoun" because the large church at the center of the burgh was dedicated to Saint John the Baptist.

Sir Law Kintour, Cormac MacEda, Dave the ratcatcher, and most of the other characters are fictional. However, there are a few historical characters in or mentioned in the novel, the most important being:

- **James I**, King of Scots.

- **Bishop Robert de Cardeny**
- **Bishop John Cameron**, Chancellor of Scotland
- **Sir William Ruthven of Balkernoch**, Lord Sheriff of the royal burgh of Perth.

ALSO BY J R TOMLIN

Sir Law Kintour Mystery Series

The Templar's Cross (Book I)

The Intelligencer (Book III)

Standalone Prequel to The Black Douglas Trilogy

Freedom's Sword

The Black Douglas Trilogy:

A Kingdom's Cost (Book I)

Countenance of War (Book II)

Not for Glory (Book III)

The Stewart Chronicles

A King Ensnared (Book I)

A King Uncaged (Book II)

A King Imperiled (Book III)

Made in the USA
San Bernardino, CA
09 May 2018